GRAVITY

CRYOBORN GIFTS

MAGGIE LYNCH

Windtree
Press

Published by Windtree Press, Portland, Oregon USA

For information about all books in the Obsidian Rim series go to: https://obsidianrim.com

Gravity: Cryborn Gifts / Maggie Lynch. -- 1st ed., Book 1 in the Obsidian Rim series

Ebook ISBN: 978-1-950387-11-3

Print ISBN: 978-1-950387-12-0

This book is dedicated to Jessa Slade. You've been on this project with me from the beginning. Your experience, your advice, your vast knowledge of science fiction and romance literature and movies has spurred me to try harder, be better, and kept me moving forward more than you'll ever know. Because of you, this book came to fruition. I've had a blast and I hope it is just the beginning of this new world.

THE OBSIDIAN RIM

Before the devastating Oblivion War, humankind had expanded from SolPrime throughout the Salty Way, exploring and settling (and sometimes exploiting and destroying; such is humankind's appetite) the many solar systems within its barred spiral arms.

They traveled in stellarships of great variety—from speedy cruisers to slow generation ships. Although humankind found no evidence of sentient alien life elsewhere in the galaxy, they adapted themselves, sometimes at great cost and danger, via genetic, cybernetic, and AI tech—to sometimes greater and sometimes lesser suitability. The stellarships conquered the vast distances with the help of Quantum Entanglement Drives, and humanity seemed poised to expand beyond our small galaxy.

That was before the Oblivion War.

The Oblivion War was the first—and last—cataclysmic intragalactic conflict. A century of battles between competing interests among the core systems was unceremoniously discontinued when the first quantum bombs were deployed. The effects of the qubition-powered bombs (q-bombs) cascaded through spacetime, resulting in the obliteration of half the galaxy and the quantum destabilization of the half that remained, pushing all survivors to the untouched farthest reaches beyond the spiral arms—the Obsidian Rim.

What is the Obsidian Rim? When the devastating waves of the oblivion bombs reached the gaseous galactic halo that marks the outer edge of the galaxy, the waves formed a scrambled magnetic field barrier that prevents QED travel beyond the Salty Way. With most of the galactic interior devastated by the Oblivion War, humanity now resides in a relatively narrow "wheel" between the destabilized dead zones consuming the spiral arms and the uncrossable starless void of intergalactic space.

Now, after the war, the survivors struggle on the Obsidian Rim, living and dying, rebuilding and losing again. In the harsher environs of the Rim, there are farmers and qubition miners, pirates and the cryoborn, but also corporate executives and self-styled royalty plus the honorable (and not so honorable) remnants of the core systems governmental structures that once ruled—and then destroyed—the galaxy.

Existence here is dark and dangerous. Looking inward, we sorrow for the past. Looking outward, we fear for the future. But on the Obsidian Rim, we fight and love for today.

"No! No, no, no," Lehana screamed as she was thrown back in the pilot seat when the qubition ejected for a third time. "What the freeze? I did not authorize that. I did not!"

A single injection of just the right amount of qubition stabilized the wormhole. But the *Phoenix* had just released her entire Q supply, enough for at least seven transits. She had no idea what that would do. At best the hole would start closing behind her and she'd exit before it closed. At worst it would collapse and she'd die. Or she'd be thrown somewhere else in the multiverse and she'd never make it back to the Salty Way.

None of those scenarios were great for a pirate who'd just changed identities, ship registration, and purloined enough credits from a systems hacker to set her up for a year without having to trade anything for income.

Painful starbursts of light exploded on the forward viewscreen. Lehana screamed again as the ship accelerated through the wormhole, seeming to fall without control toward the other side.

"Kali!" she screamed at the ships AI. "You just pissed in the vac and I'm the one who's going to pay for it. Where are we? Where can we land?"

"Calculating," the AI responded.

Lehana held back a string of additional curses as the ship shifted abruptly several more times, throwing her against the cushions of the pilot's chair until her entire body felt like she'd played with by a 500kg jellicant that rolled over her several times. It wouldn't do any good to curse at the AI. It had no feelings and had no comprehension of guilt.

"Anytime," she said to Kali through gritted teeth. "It would be nice to know where we're crashing before I pass out."

"Reverse thrust. Aligning for re-entry," Kali reported. "Fuel expended."

"What do you mean expended? We need to slow to subsonic speed! Dump the cargo bay."

"Cargo bay not releasing. Aerobraking in three...two... one...now."

Lehana was thrown back in her seat, and the increasing pressure on her chest pinned her there as the Gs climbed.

"Prepare for atmospheric re-entry in five...four....three..."

"Drakh! Drakh! Drakh!" Lehana hit the enclosure button on her chair. The padded headrest and seat back extended into a circle enclosing her in a shell that would cushion her body in the crash.

"Brace for impact," Kali instructed.

She felt the ship bounce three, no, four times along the surface of something and then impact. Everything went dark.

Lehana woke to a headache worse than the last time she'd had a hangover from a bad batch of vac-alky. Though she could see nothing in her egg cocoon, she heard all kinds of alerts and warnings heightening the pain.

Kali said, all too loudly, "Starting repairs. Estimated time for first level systems is two planetary days."

"Shut off all audible alerts," Lehana instructed, her voice a scratchy whisper as if she'd been screaming for days.

The welcoming silence helped her take a deep breath and center her thoughts. "What about second and third level repairs?" She didn't need so many noises echoing in her head. "And open my egg so I can see what the hell is going on."

"Egg opening is a second level task," Kali said without inflection. "Task scheduled on day four."

"Like hell I'm staying in here for four days. Make it a first level, high priority, right-this-minute task!"

"It will take a minimum of— "

"I. Said. Now!"

The padded egg creaked open about one third of the way.

"That is all I can manage until other first level systems are operational," Kali said.

Lehana manually released the harness holding her, and then snaked an arm out the opening. She braced her hand against the outside shell casing and groaned as she leveraged herself up to stand with one leg out and one leg inside. She balanced for a moment checking her steadiness. Though she was petite, her frame barely fit through the opening. Satisfied with her balance, she slowly extracted the other leg and arm, this time biting off a whimper.

The viewport to the front of the ship showed nothing but sand and rock. "How bad is the hull?"

"The structure is stable," Kali responded.

Was that a note of pride Lehana heard? No it couldn't be. AIs didn't show pride.

"And the cargo bay?"

"Structurally stable though repairs are needed on individual units. It is not pretty," Kali added. "Exterior repairs, outside of hole patching, are not in my purview."

Lehana sighed. Not that she cared if the ship was beautiful, but she'd just paid a good two-hundred million credits for a brand new hull. When she'd left dock on the other side of the galaxy, it had been reinforced with the latest technology and the skin honed to a nice matte finish that absorbed light instead of letting it bounce off the hull. That helped mask her travels across the Salty Way. Perhaps that investment in the hull, along with heat shield upgrades she didn't think she'd ever need, were what saved the ship.

She carefully turned from side to side and stretched. Nothing seemed broken, even though she ached from the beating of the landing. The egg had done its job.

"What the freeze happened with the Q injection? Why did you dump the entire load?" They'd had some scary wormhole traverses before but this one could have left her spaghetified and never to be found again.

"Instruction for Q injection was exact," Kali stated.

"Like hell it was. Dumping eight loads is *not* exact."

"Checking log…log states one load was injected."

"But clearly that isn't true," Lehana bit out the words as she held back the desire to pound something.

"It is false data," Kali agreed. "I will perform a full diagnostic on my injection code. Shall I give that priority over first level tasks?"

"Drakh," Lehana swore. What was an AI good for if it couldn't accurately prioritize? "We aren't injecting Q soon. We don't have any Q onboard anymore because *you* dumped your wad in the hole. So what do you think? Of course, it is not a first-level task. But you damn well better have it figured out before we get off this planet and make another jump."

"The rise in your voice indicates a level of frustration that is misplaced," Kali commented. "I am not capable of making mistakes. If there is an error, it is a human in error in my programming error and I will identify and correct it. If it makes you able to better make decisions, I will await your sting of curses before your next instruction."

Lehana paced back and forth, cursing in her mind. She was not going to let the AI tell her how to respond.

"Where, exactly, are we?" she finally asked. May it please the stars they were in friendly territory.

"Ydro-Down."

Lehana knew QueCorp, the mining company that ran Ydro-Down. Was it two or three transits ago that she'd picked up a full load of Q to deliver to a space station on the other side? "I know the station here. Have you already sent the request for assistance?"

"We are not at the primary trading station," Kali said. "Request for assistance was rejected without proof of advanced payment for a gravity lift to the catapult and payment for the catapult to space dock. The cost is one million DICs per one-hundred kilometers per ten thousand tons for the gravity assist to the catapult, and two million per ten thousand tons for cata-pult payload."

Lehana shook her head, unable to comprehend what she just heard. "I know we are not in the station. We are obviously buried in rock on the planet. But we are near the catapult station. Right?"

"Negative. We are closest to mine 154893, approximately two-hundred and seventy-four kilometers from catapult to space dock."

Lehana did a quick calculation in her head. She had approximately 5.2 million DICs left in her accounts after expenditures to get the Phoenix in shape. No way could she afford a gravity lift to the station and still be able to purchase Q to get her through the next wormhole. If she was lucky, she might negotiate a single load of Q for five million DICs. That's assuming she could get a fifty percent reduction from the current market rate, leaving her almost nothing for repairs beyond what Kali could make using what materials already on the ship.

"Will level one repairs get us airborne?" she asked. "Enough to get us to the station?"

"Negative. Level one repairs are to backups for life support, the medical bay, and sanitary systems. Level two will include significant repairs to achieve cruising control and enough escape velocity to leave the planet and get to space dock with the help of the catapult."

"Concentrate on getting us off planet. I'll work on negotiating a Q load and advanced credit for repairs."

"Estimated time five days," Kali said.

"Make it three."

"That is not possi—"

"That is not a suggestion. I can't afford to stay here any longer than three days. This is not a friendly place. It will take all my persuasive powers, and likely a good amount of bribery, just to make sure my ship isn't impounded by QueCorp. I had no permission to land and they will certainly take offense at the fact I crashed into a current or future mining line."

"I will attempt to complete needed repairs in three days," Kali affirmed.

"Not attempt. You will do it."

Kali did not respond.

CHAPTER 2

The alert of a possible cave-in had the miners scrambling toward the entrance, running into each other like ions shot into a collider. Kash had felt the earthquake while he was deep in the mine, but it was not like the usual rolling shake they endured almost daily. This felt like the time one of the whompers had hit a new vein and burst through an empty space to fall into a new cavern. He'd seen machines fall into the maw of rock when they hit a hollow spot. Often the entire floor collapsed and all those nearby died in the fall. Every time it happened, the ground shook like the planet was imploding.

His environmental suit visor darkened as they emerged from the darkness into the dusty, sun-drenched landscape. The comm whispers from other miners reached him, but he couldn't believe his ears. A starfreighter? Here? That was impossible. Starfreighters were too big to land on Ydro-Down. They docked in space and shuttled cargo and personnel down to the planet.

"Line up. No talking. Count off. If anyone is missing you all will pay by working all night." The crew chief overrode the individual comms.

The whispers silenced and each worker lined up in number order, looking like a small army of clones. All of them were sweating inside identical suits with darkened visors.

"One ninety two," Kash stated his miner identification in a clear voice when it was his turn.

He was an older miner, having been here for forty-five turns. The count off continued through the final and newest miner, number one thousand forty-four, having come of age to work only half a turn ago. He shuddered at the thought of his oldest being conscripted at age ten. Perhaps it was better his first child was kept in stasis at nearly four years old. His son would not reach age ten until released and allowed time to grow.

No one had tried to escape for at least seventeen turns of the planet. Though every one of them dreamed of escaping, it seemed futile. The few who tried had been brought back dead and displayed for all to see. There was nothing between this mine and the catapult station, the only place with any hope to stow away on a small luxury cruiser or shuttle. Only unforgiving desert, other mines, and overlords lay over the more than two-hundred seventy kilometer distance. No water. No cover from the sun or the road. Their environmental suits were issued for each shift and recovered once they entered the warren of underground caves that constituted their sleeping quarters.

The few who had tried to escape left during a shift, keeping their suit on with a plan to conserve air and energy while walking toward safety. However, word spread quickly that no one at any other mine would dare shelter a runaway or provide a new suit and filtration pack for them to continue to toward the catapult launch.

Kash had not even contemplated that type of escape. Even if there were people willing to shelter him, he could never manage the distance hauling his two children in cryounits.

Silently, Kash stared at the starfreighter embedded in the side of the mine. He could feel the unease of the men and women around him. Each one wondering if the ship could escape Ydro-Down. Each one thinking what it would take to stow away undetected. Each one wondering the size of the crew, who or what was aboard already, and if the captain was one of the few who disagreed with slavery and would at least look the other way when finding a stowaway.

It was a big freighter, certainly the largest Kash had ever seen. Not knowing how much of the length was buried in the mine, he estimated it to be at least three-hundred meters long. Certainly it was big enough to take him and his two children aboard. It must have crew quarters. Probably a med bay, too, to ease them from cryosleep. He'd be happy for the three of them to share a single space if he could manage it.

He shook his head. Don't even consider it. This ship would likely be impounded and the captain and crew either killed or made a slave like himself. At the least QueCorp would make the captain pay a hefty fine for destroying part of a mine.

"There will be no mining at this site until the ship is removed," the crew chief said through comms. "Double rations for the first thirty who volunteer to dig her out."

Kash surged forward, pushing aside other miners in order to be at the front of the line and chosen. Double rations meant many could better feed their families. For Kash, it was a beacon of hope that he could find a way to get his children onto this ship and have food for a journey of several days until they were discovered.

The crew chief pointed, one by one, to the thirty he would take. Kash was the second one chosen. The man laughed as Kash stepped up and he read the tag on his environmental suit.

"Number one ninety-two, how many rations do you have already stored for those babies?" he asked.

"Fifteen or sixteen, sir," Kash answered.

The chief laughed again. "Sixteen days rations for two half-dead children. No wonder you are a slave. You have no idea how to take care of yourself. If you were smart you'd let those children die and keep the extra rations for yourself, or trade them for other goods."

"Yes, sir," Kash responded automatically.

The chief laughed again and looked over the other fifty. "Anyone else storing rations for dead children?" All the other volunteers shook their head.

Kash knew he was different. None of the others were cryoborn. None of the others had escaped the Oblivion War in a generational ship and entered the Obsidian Rim in cryosleep when the quantum wave hit. None of the others knew what life was like a two thousand turns ago, how people lived in community and helped each other. None of them knew; and only a few even pretended to care.

In his forty-five years of mining Q no ships had ever landed at the mines. Most shuttles coming from space dock landed at the orbiting station above this mine that was tidally locked with the planetoid. The executives lived at the station and took the secure space elevator to the planets surface. When new miners were delivered, they were escorted by the guardians and never allowed on the space elevator again.

A starfreighter crashing at this particular mine was a once in a lifetime event. This might be his only chance to escape.

"One ninety-two," the crew chief said. "You will lead the effort inside the mine. Take nine miners and dig your way to the ship's bridge. Once you reach it you alert me. If you see anyone inside, you alert me. Understand?"

"Yes, sir," Kash responded.

The crew chief put his helmet against Kash's helmet for a private communication. "Your children's lives are the payment for any mistakes, any failure to keep me informed." Then he stepped back.

"Proceed," the crew chief said and pointed at the pile of shoulder bags just inside the mine. "The rest of you will work from the outside. Once we uncover the docking port and are able to board, we will know exactly what we have here."

Kash stepped forward first and slung the bag over his shoulder. It contained a 3D printer for processing iron ore to create structural supports as they dug toward the ship. When Kash and the other nine miners reached the shaft closest to the bridge of the ship, six of them took the printers and set up a spot to process the left over iron ore that had encapsulated the Q. The printer spit it out into successive strands to build the appropriate structural support. Two others set their printers to create fasteners to put the supports together.

Kash was in charge of running the whomper, a large automated digger. The next several hours were filled with the sounds of digging, followed by construction as the miners slowly moved closer and closer to the ship.

Five hours. Six. Eight. Ten. Each hour they paused for ten minutes so their suits could process their sweat and urine into a liquid they could sip to keep hydrated. Not one of the miners complained or showed outward signs of tiredness.

The possibilities of double rations and unspoken dreams of escape kept the adrenalin pumping. They all wanted to see the ship. They all wanted the same chance for freedom. Kash could see it in their eyes when they paused for their ten-minute breaks—eyes that reflected his own thoughts of escape.

"Stop digging!" one of the miners shouted. "I see the hull of the bridge."

Kash silenced the whomper and quickly moved forward to brush away small bits of dirt, revealing a large rounded piece of the hull covered in at least two inches of debris. "Careful," he said to the others. "We don't want to damage the skin."

The other nine workers surged forward with a combination of soft brushes and hand-held scrapers. Within another hour they had the majority of the window exposed to the bridge and the ship's name was emblazoned just below it: Phoenix.

Kash dropped to one knee in surprise. It was an omen. It had to be.

"Woman. Alive." Several people said it at the same time and Kash stood again to peer into the window. The interior lights were on and a petite woman stood in battle gear and stared out at them, a knife clutched in one hand as if she anticipated being taken.

Suddenly, the woman threw back her head and laughed. She secreted the knife in her vest, and then smiled and waved like a schoolgirl.

Kash's mouth dropped open.

"Call the chief. Call the chief." Several miners whispered.

For a moment, Kash wanted to say no. He wanted to talk to her. Who was this pilot with enough boldness to smile and wave without worry? Either she was wormy or she possessed the fearlessness he needed to get him and his children off this planet. He looked at the other men, all of them mesmerized by the woman's actions.

He shook his head to quarry his thoughts. Not calling it in was suicide for him and his children. He pressed the communicator on his uniform. "At the bridge. Forward view window shows pilot inside. Alive. Female."

"Other crew?" the crew chief asked.

"Not visible," Kash responded.

"Stand down," the chief ordered. "Scraff is on his way."

A shudder went through all the workers. Harris Scraff was the executive overlord of this mine. He was cruel and didn't think twice about killing anyone he thought was in his way. He gloried in making an example of someone just to put fear into the miners. If he thought they did anything wrong in uncovering the ship, he wouldn't hesitate to make someone the example.

Kash didn't envy the woman. If she survived meeting Scraff, he'd find a way to contact her and to try to negotiate his passage for his help getting her get off planet. Before Kash and his wife had been captured and enslaved on Ydro-Down, he'd had a reputation among the cryoborn as being a gifted navigator. Certainly, it was not a skill he could use here; and he'd told no one. But this time it could mean the difference between eternal slavery and freedom for him and his children, if... if he could find a way to get to this woman and convince her he would be an asset instead of a deficit.

LEHANA COULDN'T HELP but laugh at the miner's response when she'd waved. Though it was hard to see their expression through the environmental suits they wore. The way they stopped all movement was as if she had momentarily stopped time from moving forward. She figured what the hell. Whoever came to meet her was not likely to be friendly, so she might as well go down laughing. Perhaps, if they thought she was wormy —some pilots went insane after a bad transit of the wormhole— they wouldn't kill her right away.

"Darken viewport," she instructed and then quickly stripped out of her clothing and into a skinsuit that would make it easier to get into the body-hugging environmental suit she'd have to wear on planet. She was still taking weapons, in case she needed to defend herself, but they would be hidden beneath a couple of layers and hard to find in a pat down.

"Status," she said to Kali.

"Two days, three hours."

"So, you will meet my three day deadline."

"Probability is seventy two percent," Kali responded.

"I know you can do better. Optimize. I'll be comfortable at 85% or above."

"Working."

"Give me information on the executive associated with this particular mine and their customs and habits."

"QueCorp owns all mining rights on Ydro-Down. Owner is Ming Waller."

"I know that part," Lehana said. "I've traded with QueCorp plenty of times over the years. Ming and I go way back. I want to know who is likely to come greet me at this particular mine. Friend or foe? Should I shoot first or shake the individual's hand or, stars forbid, give a kiss of some type?"

"Overly friendly foe, named Harris Scraff."

"Ohhhh, I remember him. Handsy. Privileged. Can be cruel when provoked. But he can be manipulated."

"Records indicate on your last encounter he tried to kill you by strangulation."

"Yes, I remember that well." Lehana rubbed the side of her neck. She'd sported a bruise for a good week after that. Scraff was one of those men who would not take no as an answer and didn't care if he killed the woman in the process. When she didn't accept his advances he thought he would subdue her by cutting off her air and doing whatever he wanted.

Lehana had been raped when she was barely thirteen. It took her three months to get up the courage to tell Hellebor about it. He found the man who did it and killed him, slowly. Not because he loved Lehana or was loyal to her, but because she was his property and no one touched his property without permission. After that she learned self-defense. She learned to become the aggressor. She studied how to stop things before they started by showing she was willing to kill too.

She'd knifed Scraff in the side and escaped while he fell to the ground and bled profusely. She'd hoped she'd killed him, but evidently not.

She doubted he would recognize her though. She'd had blonde hair then, with hints of grey, an aquiline nose and blue eyes. She'd designed herself to look to be in her forties, mistakenly believing that would dissuade casual seduction attempts. She'd also been considerably taller and heavier. What was her identity then? Avia? Zallili? She couldn't remember. That was at least three nanobot changes ago and twenty-eight yearunits.

With her latest image regeneration she'd made her hair dark, shrunk four inches, lost forty pounds, and redid her face to be that of someone in her twenties. Though younger women caused more unwanted advances, she could also use it to distract and manipulate if needed. If Scraff had heard of Lehana Saar it was only in glowing terms as the best Q trader in the galaxy, or maybe as a keen negotiator and a bit of a party girl. Ming Waller trusted her to always get his deliveries to customers on time and under budget. Because she took chances no one else dared, Ming always gave her first choice on the longest and most dangerous deliveries. He also paid her handsomely, with the bonus of triple pay compared to what other Q traders received for their easy deliveries.

If things went well, she'd negotiate a Q delivery and the ability to get off this dust ball with her ship intact. And maybe even more money in her accounts.

She pushed a button in the console and retrieved a tranquilizer dart, secreting it in the sleeve just above her left wrist. She'd be prepared this time. Scraff would likely try to be more persuasive with a younger woman, and choking was not going to happen again.

Lehana checked her skinsuit to make sure her knife, ray gun, and choke-ties were well hidden before donning the environmental suit. Then she swiftly headed toward the docking door that was the only passenger access to the ship.

"Send a message to QueCorp at space dock," she instructed as she walked. "Tell them Lehana Saar is here to do business, and I will make a good bargain in return for getting me and the *Phoenix* out of this mine in one piece."

"Visitors at docking door," Kali announced at the same time Lehana arrived.

She stood with her feet wide apart, ready for multiple possibilities. ""It's show time. Open the door."

The docking door unlocked and hinged inward.

A miner stood in front of her staring.

"I'm the...uh...bait in case you come out shooting." His voice held no fear. In fact, it seemed he was nonchalant about the possibility of being dead right now.

"No weapons," Lehana stated, her arms slightly away from her side, palms outward.

The miner approached and stood within twenty centimeters of her. She swallowed, preparing for any eventuality. Now that she saw him up close, his suit was not only covered in the sticky dirt of this star-forsaken planetoid, but the frayed edges clearly indicated it was on the edge of failure. He wiped the back of his hand across his visor and she could see his face. His lips were firmly together; his jaw held tight. But his wide-open, dark blue eyes stared straight at her. The hints of gold specs in the iris appeared like tiny stars against the deep blue field.

She took a step through the door and her ankle wobbled to one side as her foot caught on a rock.

The miner placed a steadying hand below her elbow and she grabbed tight to him as a strange current quickly ran through her suit followed by a flash of bright light, momentarily blinding her.

The miner gasped and stumbled backward into one of the guardians, who roughly pushed him away toward the other miners standing behind him.

Lehana quickly regained her balance and took a deep breath to calm her racing pulse. What the vac was that? And why did it effect the miner as well. Some kind of scanner? Had he been instructed to disorient her in some way?

"Get on with your business," an abrasive voice said to the miners. They scrambled in different directions, leaving her alone with two guardians pointing guns directly at her.

Then Scraff strode forward. It was true to form that he let others clear the way and protect him before exerting himself. He appeared much the same as she remembered him. His eyes scanned her slowly, and a small grin started on one side of his mouth. Obviously, his lascivious nature hadn't changed over the years. Good, she could use that against him.

"So, this is how you greet a stranded Q trader?" she asked Scraff with a hint of seduction in her voice.

"Protocol," Scraff said in a surly voice. "Take her to my quarters, strip her and frisk her for weapons. Then hold her there until I arrive."

Lehana held up a hand. "Not so fast, now. I suggest you wait ten shakes." She heard the comm signal come to Scraff's device. "That will be a call from QueCorp."

Scraff looked at his comm and blanched as he noted the sender.

She cocked her head and smiled behind her visor.

"Delay my order but keep your guns trained on her," he said, and then stood straight, as if someone had pushed a rod down his spine. He tapped twice beside his ear so that no one else would hear what was said from corporate.

"Yes, sir, Mr. Waller."

Lehana waited through each silent pause with a cocky smile as Waller spoke to Scraff.

"I understand…Yes, sir. No damage to her…We are greeting her now…Dignitary protocol. Yes, sir. I will, sir."

He tapped his ear again and then shouted at the guardians. "Stand down. Dignitary protocol." Then he approached with his right hand offered. "My apologies, Captain Saar. We've never had any kind of ship crash on Ydro-Down before. I just assumed…" He cleared his throat. "I…uh… understand you are a good friend of Mr. Waller and a trusted Q trading partner. Again, my apologies for treating you like a common…"

"Thief?" Lehana asked, her eyebrow raised. "I'm far more dangerous than any common thief."

Scraff swallowed and cleared his throat again. "May I escort you to my quarters? There you can refresh yourself and, with your permission, we can share a meal while QueCorp is working on how to help your ship get back underway as quickly as possible."

She accepted his hand in a single quick shake and formed a thin-lipped smiled. She well-remembered his quarters and, before she left this time, she would take something precious from him. Something that might help repay what he did to her previously.

CHAPTER 3

Kash paced his small room. He was not giving up, even though it was evident the captain of that freighter was in the pocket of QueCorp. Waller was the owner of the entire corporation with mining interests across several planetoids and asteroids in the Rim. With friends like that, she wouldn't need any help getting off planet. In fact, there was nothing Kash could offer to entice her to help him. He needed a different plan. Unfortunately, a more dangerous plan.

He placed his hand on the cryounit window where his son, Eijaz, slept peacefully only steps from Kash's cot. Eijaz had known only three and a half years of being alive. Though living here as the child of miners did not allow for much freedom, he had taken it in stride, finding joy in discoveries within this room and on his twice weekly journeys to the bathing stations where he could play freely in actual water for three minutes. He also loved putting on the environmental suit for his twice a month journey outside for the twenty minutes allowed for acclimating children to the suits and the heat they would be required to endure beginning at age ten.

Watching Eijaz be put in cryosleep was the hardest thing Kash had ever done, next to watching his wife die. It was then he'd made the promise to himself that Eijaz would awake to better circumstances and a chance to truly be free. Most of all, he would make sure Eijaz would never become a miner.

He turned to the smaller cryounit with his six-month old daughter, Z-Huang. He had only held the baby four or five times before his wife died in his arms. She'd made it through the childbirth, but then slowly wasted away over six months. All of her energy had gone to nursing the child and making sure she would survive.

Q had a reputation for depleting the immune system of pregnant women. Though there were decontamination procedures for everyone exiting the cave, most suits had pinhole leaks that allowed some Q dust to enter the environmental suit. QueCorp didn't care what it did to women. They saw it as a good punishment for them getting pregnant and being unable to work for extended periods of time.

Huang's first birth with Eijaz had seen no side effects and once she knew she was pregnant with Eijaz she stopped going into the mines. However, she was required to return to work when Eijaz turned two. She and Kash took opposite shifts so someone would always be with the child.

She had no idea she was pregnant the second time until six months into her term. By then it was too late when she discovered a pinhole tear in her suit. She didn't know how long it had been there. The second birth had been more difficult and her system had fully metabolized the Q. It was only her sheer will to do everything to ensure the baby's safety that made her live six months after the birth. Many women died in childbirth when exposed to Q.

The medics had put both Z-Huang and Eijaz in cryosleep within moments of his wife's last breath. No one knew how babies fared in long-term cryosleep. No one could say how much of the Q had been passed to the baby through the mother and what impacts it would have on her. Kash feared she may be forever impaired in some way. But it didn't matter. He would care for her no matter her abilities.

"Z-Huang, I promise you will live again," he vowed in a whisper. Then added in his mind: away from Ydro-Down. All the miners' rooms were monitored continuously. He didn't dare voice even the hope of escape one day.

He put his head to the cryounit window and kissed it before turning away and crawling into bed, curling into a tight ball as if the tension could keep any thought of failure out of his dreams.

His wife had named the baby Zia to honor Kash's heritage and his request to keep the meaning of his wife's name: light-shining-luminous. But after her death he wanted—no, he needed—to have his wife's named remembered, spoken aloud regularly. Huang in the feminine meant not only light-filled, but also invoked the ancient bird, the Phoenix. The one who dies in fire but rises again from the ashes. Though his wife would not rise from the ashes of Ydro-Down, he could ensure that her name and her soul would live again through his daughter.

And now it appeared the universe had given him a chance to fulfill his promise. A ship named Phoenix. It was as if Huang had sent him this chance to save the children. It might never come again in his lifetime.

Kash woke early. He needed help, and the only person he might be able to trust was Gavyn Grey. He spoke a quick message for Gavyn into the com link.

:Msg. Miner 488

Gavyn, up for CW3? After tomorrow's shift? My fingers are aching to play.:

A message came back quickly.

:Msg. Miner 192

Yes. Mine? Or Cave?:

Kash replied quickly.

:Msg. Miner 488

Cave.:

:Msg. Miner 192

SYT:

Kash breathed a sigh of relief. He'd be meeting Gavyn in the game cave after tomorrow's shift. The cave always had multiple players, making it noisy. Sometimes very public places were the best place to carry out private conversations. Now he had to hope the game grid was conducive to asking the questions he needed.

Gavyn was the closest thing to a friend Kash had. No one on Ydro-Down made real friends. It wasn't safe. Anyone could be a QueCorp spy looking for potential uprisings or to test your loyalty by offering freedom in exchange for rations or anything one could barter. However, Kash believed Gavyn wasn't a QueCorp spy. He hoped his intuition would be proven right because today he was going to bet his own life and the life of his children on asking for Gavyn's help to stowaway on the Phoenix.

When Huang was dying, Gavyn had been among only a few

miners who offered their condolences. He was the only miner who visited Kash and seemed to understand his grief both in losing his wife and seeing his children cryoed.

Every day for a month Gavyn visited after his shift in the mine. He was a big man, easily a head taller than Kash and at least twenty percent heavier in pure muscle. Fitting his large frame into Gavyn's hovel was not easy.

For the first week he was just there—sitting in silence with Kash, offering a quiet presence. After two or three hours Gavyn would simply leave. The second week he taught Kash a way to use the common CS3 game to speak his feelings without fear of reprisals from Scraff.

CS3 was a popular 3D holographic game based on the two ancient earth games of Crossword and Scrabble. The 21 x 21 grid on each face of the CS3 cube provided possibilities for words to intersect in one plane, as well as spill over to the other plane. The AI would build the grid. Twenty-four hours in advance, each player would begin preparing half of the clues. One player provided the even numbered clues, while the other player provided the odd numbered clues.

Over the next few months of playing together, Kash began to notice a pattern of clues related to Gavyn's nervous tapping. Sometimes it was a few toe taps, other times it was a finger tap. Then he realized Gavyn was training him to use CS3 to learn a new, secret language to communicate. For example, if the previous clue was: a pirate's body part replaced with a stick; the correct word to put on the cube might be leg. Gavyn's next clue was: unknown rest time, followed by three finger taps. The finger taps meant the related clue was on the third plane of the cube and the word was important to their coded communication: cryosleep.

Slowly they worked together to create this secret communication pattern using language relating to finger taps, toe taps, stretching, scratching the chin and many other slight body movements. Eventually, they could briefly comment on rumors, make plans to steal an extra ration of water, or exchange environmental suits to take the other's shift when needed.

If Gavyn had a plan, Kash needed it now before the *Phoenix* rose from the planet.

CHAPTER 4

On the second day of her ship's repairs, Lehana dressed casually for breakfast. When she didn't see Scraff already seated at the table, she breathed a sigh of relief. Since his discussion with the owner yesterday, he had been the perfect host. They had a reasonable dinner together with him drinking too much vac-alky and she eating far too much of his gourmet feast of fresh vegetables, actual root potatoes, and something that tasted like synth mackerel but couldn't possibly be. As far as she knew there was no planet in the Rim that had enough water to support a fish population. But the taste was amazing and, when she closed her eyes, she could imagine it had come from one of Earth's original sources sent with the generational ships. Even on the pirate outposts where they could afford any luxury, she hadn't had such a good tasting fish substitute.

It was just his arrogance, his obvious narcissism, and his complete disregard for the miners that had her biting her tongue all the time. He talked freely because he assumed she had the same outlook on life. She didn't. It was true she never stuck her neck out for anyone. But that wasn't because she thought they were unworthy. It was that she had learned the hard way not to trust and not to get attached. That only brought pain, and could even mean death.

Though she would never risk her life to fight against the enslavement of miners, she didn't agree with it. Her own fifty turns of indentured service with the great pirate, Hellebor, was very rough but at least he was fair and predictable. She also knew there was an end to it. As long as she turned everything over to Hellebor, she was also well-compensated with her fair share of any profits. That was the pirate's code. Sure her portion was small as an indentured servant, but once freed she had the option of staying and getting a larger share on all ongoing missions he ran. She chose to leave. She was given twenty million DICs in her account, and the training to be a great negotiator, a quick-minded and careful thief, and one of the best pilots in the quadrant. Unfortunately, that wasn't enough to buy a ship. She stole Hellebor's luxury cruiser, headed to the first wormhole and dumped it on the other side, trading up. Not the most brilliant of choices. She could have stolen a ship from a different band, but she was impatient. She wanted out immediately.

She sighed. That was behind her. Hellebor would never find her and his ship was long gone. At least she'd had a choice. The miners had nothing but a life of knowing this was where they would live and die.

That wasn't right. But it also wasn't her problem.

Her comm dinged and she flipped it to privacy mode with the information displayed in her glass and the audio input going directly to her ear.

"Contact from Ming Waller," Kali relayed.

Lehana relaxed into the chair in the guest bedroom. The last thing she wanted was to show she was anxious to hear from him. "Connect," she said to Kali.

"Ming, how considerate of you to call me yourself."

The well-dressed man smiled easily. "Lehana Saar, it seems you've put yourself in a difficult position this time."

"How difficult it is remains to be seen," she replied as she raised her hand slightly to one side, indicating it wasn't that big a deal. "I do apologize for running into one of your mines. It was not intentional."

"And what would you have me do?" Ming asked, his smile now turning into more of a smirk. "Dig you out, dust you off, and let you go on your way with no consequence?"

Lehana sighed audibly. "I'm not asking for that at all. I know there is payment. The question is how much and what can we negotiate. Last time we met, you were looking at a delivery of Q in the dead zone. No trader in her right mine would enter that area—even me. Spacetime has been so warped from the Q-bombs that there is less than a ten percent chance of returning. You would lose me and your cargo."

"The cargo being the more valuable," Ming said.

She laughed. "To you perhaps."

Ming leaned forward until his entire face filled her screen. "Are you suggesting you are now willing to take the run?"

"Perhaps," she said, drawing out the word, making an effort not to shrink into her chair at his serious presence. The look in his eye was now one of a predator instead of a friendly negotiator. "Is the payment still ten times the usual delivery? Fifty million DICs for delivery, one hundred million for hazard pay for me and my crew, and no lien on my accounts if I fail?"

"If you fail, you and your crew will be dead, so what do you care about a lien?"

"I have a charity or two I'd like to see helped."

Ming threw his head back and laughed for a full minute before catching his breath. "You? A charity? Never. We both know you are all about profit and have no feelings for anyone or anything other than yourself."

"You make me sound so cold," she responded with feigned offense. "I do have a soft spot for medical scholarships. It's so hard to find a good medic who enjoys traversing the wormhole regularly."

"I'm sure it's hard for you to find any crew loyalty. Your reputation for changing out crews every turn is legendary."

"Enough about me." Lehana straightened and put on her game face. "I'm sending you my offer. Fifty million delivery within a quarter turn, one hundred million bonus after proof of delivery. No liens on my accounts."

"I accept the fifty million direct payment and the one hundred million bonus, however there will be liens for the repairs on your ship, the gravity assist to get your ship to the catapult, and the use of the catapult. Or had you forgotten the Phoenix cannot escape Ydro-Down without my help?"

"My AI is making good progress on repairs," Lehana countered.

"And how long will that take?" Ming asked. "Half a turn? An entire turn? Did I mention I would normally fine a ship by the day? I'd let that go because it is you. But perhaps I should rethink that."

"Thanks for such a kind thought," Lehana said, her head shaking back and forth to show her surprise. "Obviously you have a number in mind for all this assistance. What might that be?"

"I'm sending the full bill now."

She took a moment to scan to the bottom line. "Really? Only

five hundred sixty million? Only three times your actual public costs?"

Ming chuckled. "You haven't lost your edge, after all."

"If anything, I have more edge. Let's get real. I know your normal charge for gravity assist for my size ship is one hundred thirty million DICs, and the catapult is two hundred thirty six million. Why would you try to stiff one of your best Q traders?"

"Because you crashed into my mine," he said, raising his voice. "There is payment for that, the lost work hours. It all goes to profit. My profit. "

"Understood," Lehana said slowly. "But I'm offering to make a delivery that you know will get you a minimum of a billion DICs and I'm the one taking all the risks. If I don't do it, no one will do it and you know it. Why hasn't it been delivered in the past two years since I turned it down?"

Silence.

After a full minute she said, "Exactly. I'm the only one able to do it."

"I'm losing profit every day your ship is at that mine, not to mention the miner unrest you've created."

"The more reason for you to get me moved quickly."

"Two hundred eighty million and the lien on your account for that amount until you have proof of delivery. Final offer."

Lehana quickly calculated how that would work. She'd get the fifty million now which she could immediately apply against the repair and off-planet assist. She couldn't count on the hundred million at all. Not that Ming wasn't good for it; she wasn't sure she'd survive to collect. In fact, she might decide at the last minute not to chance going into the dead zone at all. She'd do some reconnaissance at a safe distance and then decide.

No way was she allowing him to have access to her

accounts, dead or alive. She'd worked hard for what she had and she would need her two hundred million DICs reserve if she ran into any further trouble or had to do an identity or ship change.

"I could just send the guardians to arrest you and keep you here on Ydro-Down," Ming reminded her. "This is a fair offer."

"You could try," Lehana said. "That is if you want to deal with Hellebor. He is a close, very personal friend."

"I don't believe it. That pirate is a friend to no one. Even you aren't crazy enough to run with him."

"You think so?" She turned to one side and showed a tattoo on her left shoulder. "Do you recognize the mark?"

She heard Ming's intake of breath.

"I do," he said softly.

"I was raised by him from age six. I was with his gang for fifty turns prior to becoming independent. It's not something I share with anyone, and I suggest you keep it to yourself."

"That explains everything." His voice mixed with awe and anger. "Danger is second nature to you. Stealing, killing is second nature to you."

"I plead guilty to the danger part," she confirmed. "Stealing and killing not so much. I did do those things with him. It was a matter of survival, but I choose not to do them now unless my life is danger." She waited for several seconds. "Is my life or my freedom in danger now?"

She watched the swallow of his throat. "No." He attempted a chuckle. "Come on, Lehana, you know it's all negotiable."

"For me, my life or my freedom is not negotiable. Ever."

Ming nodded once.

Lehana leaned forward now. "This is my final offer, and it is fair because no matter what a pirate does, it is with a code of honor and fairness." She held up her index finger. "We are agreed on the fifty million upfront payment for me to take the Q to the dead zone for delivery."

She held up a second finger. "We are agreed that you will pay a one hundred million DIC bonus upon receiving proof of delivery, and that will be done within a quarter turn."

She held up a third finger. "We are agreed that the costs for getting my ship to the catapult and using the catapult will be two hundred thirty six million. You know that is the right price, so don't bump it up."

"But—"

She held up a fourth finger. "Fourth, we are agreed that in recognition of your additional costs and loss of miner productivity for four days, I will take a fifty million DICs deduction from the bonus."

She held up her thumb. "Finally, there will be no lien on my accounts. The risk is mutual. If I die, I lose everything—my life, the lives of my crew, my ship. You also lose your Q load. That is fair. There is no recovery from me after death."

Lehana waited as Ming sat stiffly, saying nothing. She would wait hours if that was required.

She didn't mean to bring up Hellebor. It just came out from habit. The one thing she couldn't tolerate was someone threatening her freedom. She'd worked fifty turns for that. In reality, the last thing she wanted was for Hellebor to know where she was—more importantly who she was now. She'd stolen his ship when she left. The only reason he gave up looking is because she'd changed her identity and other ships too many time for him to catch up. No way would Hellebor help her or stand by her side.

She hoped Ming was scared enough of him never to contact him. She'd been careful since leaving Kollaiyar—the home world of Hellebor's crews. Maybe, once she'd delivered the Q and got the next fifty million she'd find herself a nice backwater planet on the other side of the galaxy to change her identity once again and settle into some semblance of family life. Hellebor would never find her there. He'd never believe she could do the family thing.

"I accept your conditions," Ming finally said, interrupting her thoughts. "I checked with the progress of the Phoenix and we've scheduled the gravity assist move to the catapult tomorrow. You will be informed in the morning as to the exact time of departure."

"And the fifty million advance?" Lehana asked.

"It is in your account now."

She quickly checked and then smiled. "As always, it is a pleasure doing business with you."

Ming signed off without a response.

She wanted to dance around the room. Not the best of deals she'd ever negotiated but at least she'd get off Ydro-Down with her ship, a load of Q, and fifty million DICs. She turned to the closet and started packing her things, ready to return to the ship first thing in the morning.

Her bags sat at the door, ready to go except the change of clothes for the morning. Now, there was only one more thing to do. Determine what would she take from Scraff to exact her revenge.

She walked quietly around the main living space, taking into account all the nice things Scraff had displayed on tables and shelves. Which would be his favorite? She wouldn't try to steal it. That would be too obvious and might cause Ming to give her a slap on the wrist, or worse charge her for it. Maybe she could accidentally break something. She couldn't be held responsible for an accident.

Just as she began to reach for a particularly beautiful glass vase seated on a waist-high table, a small furry animal delicately jumped onto the table without a sound. It weaved its petite body around the vase as if protecting it and then lay on the table and curled up to nap.

Lehana had never seen such an animal. It consisted of primarily dark black fur, but with a splash of brown mottled highlights along the spine, and that same color duplicated as a splash of brown and gold that spread from the forehead to the bridge of the beast's nose. The wide gold-speckled eyes had a slightly upward slant to them at the outer edges. The furry core was somewhat cylindrical, but firm, with a tail almost along as it's body. Four delicate legs with small paws supported it. The fact it could jump from the floor to the table with ease, and not rock the vase spoke of some hidden muscles and a dexterity for balance and calculating distance with ease.

She reached to touch the fur to determine if it was soft or prickly. Her hand cautiously stroked down the spine. The fur was silky beneath her fingers. The animal turned on its side and rubbed its head into her palm as if asking for more.

"I see you've found my most prized possession," Scraff said from behind her, as he reached around her to pet the animal, trapping her between him and the table.

She hadn't heard him come in, she'd been so distracted by this beast. It took every bit of willpower she had not to stomp on his instep and turn to finish him with a blow to his throat. Instead she continued to stroke the animal's head. It had a calming effect on her anger. "I've never seen such a creature."

"It is a cat," he said. "You don't see them because they are nearly impossible to acquire. This one cost me thirty-eight million DICs and the life of one of my best agents."

"Really?" Lehana drew at the word in awe. Perhaps she had found exactly what she would steal form him. She smiled at the thought. "Why would anyone pay such a dear price for an animal. Do you plan to eat it when it is larger? Is it a delicacy?"

Scraff gently lifted the cat from the table and cradled it in his arm like a baby, as he walked to settle himself in a lounge with the cat in his lap. He continued to stroke its head. "No one would ever eat a cat. That would be profane. They are the ultimate companion. Loyal, loving, never questioning your decisions or your morals. All she asks in return is food, water, and a warm place to sleep."

Lehana cocked her head, unable to match the behavior she was seeing here to the man she knew. He was so gentle, even careful with the tiny seemingly helpless animal. Certainly he could kill it with just one squeeze. The man she knew—the man all those on Ydro-Down knew—was a cruel tyrant over the miners. He was a man who wouldn't think twice about killing a human man, woman, or child if it suited his needs. He had already said he'd lost a good agent to acquire this beast and he didn't blink an eye at that loss. But he was treating this animal like some diety of old.

Perhaps this particular animal had some special magic, some kind of chemical or scent that activated a neurotransmitter in the brain like norepinephrine. That must be it, a calming effect or a mood enhancer. If that was true, having the animal might be a type of weapon he used. To own such a unique weapon would be well worth the thirty-eight million DICs he paid. The question was exactly how did it work and did it work on everyone.

"I see you are intrigued," Scraff said. "She has a name. It is Layla. It means beautiful, dark woman."

Now Lehana was even more confused. Who named an animal, or a weapon for that matter? The fact he had chosen a female gendered animal didn't surprise her, but that he gave it the dignity of a name and referred to it with a gender pronoun was remarkable. All of the slaves weren't given names, only numbers.

"Where does one find such a beast?" she asked. "I would like to acquire one. Or would you like to sell this one?"

He pulled the cat into him and obscured all but the head from her view. "I would never sell Layla at any price." Then he stared at Lehana with evil in his eyes—the same evil she'd seen the day he'd tried to strangle her. "And I would kill anyone who would even consider taking her."

She laughed to lessen the tension. "No animal is worth dying over. I can't imagine it is so precious to you. I've never known any man to prefer a beast over a human."

"They are much better than any human," Scraff said. "Humans are filled with lies, betrayals, cruelty. You can't count on them for anything. But Layla is all love and trust. She is worth a hundred humans together."

"A prize indeed," Lehana said. "As you are unwilling to sell this one, where might I find one of my own?"

The animal made a mewing sound and he released it. It jumped down and scampered into another room.

She was surprised Scraff allowed such independence. This was an unusual beast. Perhaps taking this cat would soothe her need for vengeance.

Since that first rape, she'd allowed no one to touch her without her permission. She'd permanently disabled penises in the past when someone tried to take her against her will. But she hadn't had time for that with Scraff. Though she preferred to do that, to make sure he never forced another individual, she couldn't risk it now and expect to get off Ydro-Down with her ship intact and perhaps a contract for a Q delivery. If this cat was his most prized possession, taking it from him would come close to a fair trade...for now.

"Is there a particular planet I should visit?" she asked, forcing herself to be the best type of fawning guest.

"They are occasionally found on planets where ancient generational ships landed and colonized. The Earth Conservatory might have some. Most of those old colonies don't want to be found. They brought the animals from Earth and across the Salty Way over thousands of years. Now they have built an amazing breeding program on several planets in the Rim, creating a healthy and diverse population. Raeaa is the center of this program."

"Then why the high price?" Lehana asked. "If they are plentiful, why charge so much?"

"Ah. But they are not plentiful. They need space to roam and stimulation to satisfy their curiosity, and they do not adapt well to new planets. Cats are not allowed to be removed from the planet where it is raised except for a certified breeding program. But one can always find someone to get it for you—for a price."

Lehana smiled. "Of course. DICs can buy anything."

"Exactly." He leaned forward as if to share a secret. "It took three turns for someone to locate her and make the deal. Someone on the planet was bribed to claim he was wanting the cat for his family. When my agents came to get the cat, one of them was killed. If caught stealing a cat, the punishment is death."

"And the man who was bribed?" she asked.

"Also dead," Scraff said with a fling of his finger. "Arranging for a cat to be taken off planet is also punishable by death."

That made her decision. She was definitely taking the cat with her when she left. She wasn't sure how, but she would find a way. If he risked the death of his agents and that much in DICs it was definitely his most prized possession.

For a moment she wondered how the cat would handle the transit of the wormhole. Evidently it handled it at least once before when Scraff acquired it, so she had to assume it could again. Not that it mattered in the end. What mattered is that he didn't have it.

"What are your plans today?" Scraff asked.

"I'll be taking in supplies on the ship. QueCorp has kindly supplied me with a crew to complete the level three repairs and load supplies for the medical bay, food stores, and crew quarters entertainment. Then, I understand, you have tasked shifts of miners to load the Q cargo tomorrow morning into the the four aft cargo bays."

"Yes, all the miners are at your disposal. We can't continue mining until you leave. No offense."

"None taken," she said. "If everything goes as planned, the gravity assist will begin at noon and we should be in the catapult before darkness falls."

Scraff stood. "I wish you a good flight. I will not be here to in the morning to see you off. Mr. Waller has scheduled a shuttle for me to the spacedock. I am to supervise the transfer of new miners."

"That is unfortunate. Thank you for your assistance in this unfortunate manner."

He nodded and left the room. Soon she heard him exit the building. Things just got easier. Taking the cat shouldn't be a big deal then. Too bad she couldn't scoop up a good number of unfortunate slaves he managed. That would really piss him off.

She shook her head and laughed at the thought. Don't get involved, she told herself. It was never profitable. Martyrs are those who give up on winning.

CHAPTER 5

Gavyn and Kash met in the cave after shift end as agreed. As the game started, Kash was once again amazed at the delicate touch Gavyn had when turning or tapping the cube. For such a big guy, he'd expected less finesse. But then there was a lot about Gavyn that went against type.

Kash had designed five clues in advance to frame his question. Gavyn would have to then design his answers for Kash with good clues during the second half of the game. It took an hour for Gavyn to find and put together the five coded words Kash had prepared: children, stars, Phoenix, vacation, and strategy. Gavyn nodded in understanding after getting the final one.

They struggled together as Kash solved the clues Gavyn had to come up with on the fly, while still maintaining the intersection of all the other words on the grid. Gavyn won handily in points, but Kash had managed to get the coded words for the plan: pack, exchange, squad, energy, Trojan. All but one word made sense to Kash. What did he mean by squad? Were there others Gavyn was playing this coded game with? Others who could be trusted?

Gavyn stood first and combed hair from his forehead with his hand. "I'm beat. Long day. Hard game.

Kash stood and shook Gavyn's large hand. He held on a microsecond longer than usual. This might be the last time they played. "Good game. You smashed me, again," he said with a slight lift of a smile on his lips.

"A lot more practice," Gavyn said. "I play with more competitors than you do."

"You have lots of friends here who play?"

Gavyn shrugged his shoulders. "I don't know what a lot might mean. Enough to give me plenty of games to play with known, trusted competition."

Kash couldn't help but raise his eyebrows. He'd never guessed there was any organized group looking for rebellion on this planet. Or was he reading too much into Gavyn's statement?

"Maybe I could meet a couple of them and get more practice."

"Maybe," Gavyn hedged. "There is a lot going on over the next couple of days, what with that crashed ship and getting her ready to leave. I've heard it's going take two shifts for most of us to get her in place for a gravity lift. I think you and I are on deck for loading Q in the cargo, along with some exo suits and general ship stores. Some of the others on our shift are gamers too. After the Phoenix moves out we can all recover from these doubleshifts. Then, we'll see if we have any time for more games."

Kash swallowed hard. Gavyn, and who knew how many others, were going to risk themselves to help him and his children get away. Where would the blame fall once they were gone? What would be the punishment? Could he live with the knowledge that someone might die in helping him escape?

Gavyn punched him lightly in the shoulder. "Hey, don't take it so hard. You'll have a chance to win again. When that ship is out of here, we can all celebrate."

Kash nodded and held himself tight, not trusting anything he might say now.

"See you at the mine," Gavyn said. "It's likely to be a rough day. Lots of complications. Things will have to move fast. Be prepared for anything and act without question to solve the problems."

THE NEXT MORNING, before heading out to the mine, Kash checked his messages. Gavyn had sent another congratulatory note.

:Msg. Miner 192

Good game last night. My strategy is in place for the next one. No time tonight. Pulling double shift. You better be ready to practice for next time. The Trojan is coming.:

He stared, unable to move. Did that mean someone from the squad was getting everything set up tonight? But he wouldn't be here. He'd be pulling that shift with Gavyn. He quickly wrote back.

:Msg. Miner 488

Your strategy better be air tight. Any wrong clues or answers and it is instant death.:

A message came back quickly.

:Msg. Miner 192

Don't be so dramatic. It's just a game. You'll catch on and you may even win. Who knows? Whatever happens, the game will be over in a couple days. Then we'll see if we need a rematch.:

Kash tried to get a couple hours of shuteye before his upcoming shift, but tossed and turned in his cot.

Two dark shapes appeared in his room in full environmental suits and laid down each of the cryounits.

Kash jumped from the cot, fists flying. "What the freeze?"

The first one ducked his fists and the second one wrapped an arm around his neck, choking him. "Calm down," he heard behind the visor. "Were with Gavyn."

Kash relaxed his body and nodded his assent.

The individual pointed for him to stand back.

The two of them then worked together in silence. One slipped a disk into the embedded camera that would put the vid of the cryounits on a one-hour loop. Each unit's alarms were set to silent, then the power packs quickly removed so that the signal to the company monitors would remain constant. An independent power pack was placed into each cryounit and then the units were carefully placed on the floor.

Two more individuals entered the room with a four and a half square meter cargo box labeled 'crew quarters exo suits and vid entertainment supplies'. They unloaded the items in the box and then loaded the two cryounits inside, buffering them with the blanket from Kash's cot.

Kash held up his hand before they put the crew supplies on top to hide the units. He kneeled near the box, his eyes misting as he wondered if he was sending his children to their deaths. He kissed the window of each of the cryounits and silently said a blessing he'd learned as a child. *May the stars see us all to safety.*

One of the individuals, gently removed Kash's hand from Z-Huangs unit and lifted him to a standing position, pointing him back to the cot. Then they molded three of the exo suits on top and around the units. They handed the other three suits to Kash and mimed hiding them. Kash stuffed two into the small closet and one under his cot.

The four miners then carried the box out of the room. Kash stood stiffly in one corner of his room, struggling to keep breathing. When he could no longer hear them in the hall he slid down the wall, sitting with his head between his knees.

We will be free, one way or another, he said in his mind as he thought of his wife and all the schemes they had made to leave Ydro-Down. He knew she would understand the risk he was taking and accept it gladly. If she'd been here she would have eagerly crawled in the box with the children and not made a sound of protest or fear.

He stood abruptly. He had to move. He had to get out of this room. He had to *do* something. He quickly dressed in his environmental suit and then strode with all the confidence he could muster to the cargo staging area where he would be assigned his duties. No one ever complained when a miner checked in early for a shift.

Kash watched as large boxes were removed with a forklift and taken through the sand and rocks to the *Phoenix*. Which one carried his children? He fisted his hands to stop them from opening every box to double check his children were still safe.

A second forklift arrived and stopped in front of him. The driver stepped out and tapped Kash on the shoulder. Kash looked closely at the uniform. Miner 488. Gavyn! Thank the stars.

Gavyn pointed to a stack of four large boxes, all the same size as the one that left his quarters not that long ago. "This goes into the crew quarter storage, not the primary ship's cargo. Take over the delivery and drop me back at the ship."

Kash nodded once and his breathing picked up as he moved

to climb into the machine's cabin and take the controls. He carefully worked the forks under the four stacked boxes. Just like every other load, he told himself. Nothing different.

"Nice and easy," Gavyn said into his comm as he secured the boxes to the lift with heavy cords. Then he climbed in beside Kash. "Let's get this onboard."

Kash took a deep breath and lifted the boxes, cradling them at a slight angle. He backed away from the staging area, turned in a one-hundred-eighty degree circle and headed across the one kilometer path to the ship's loading bay.

"Take a few breaths," Gavyn said, his voice calm and without much inflection. "You've been working a lot of hours. Keep a steady pace and we will get everything loaded and this ship on its way. Then we can all relax for a while."

Air whooshed out of Kash's mouth. He hadn't realized he was still holding that first breath. He breathed deeply a couple of times and nodded.

Before he could worry further they were already at the loading bay.

An individual held up a stop sign and gestured for Kash to lower the lift so the tags could be checked against the manifest. His hands gripped the controls so hard it caused the lift to shutter a bit as he started to lower the load.

"Easy," Gavyn said. "I know your tired. You can do this."

Kash nodded and completed the task without further problems.

The inspector checked tags. "Deliver to bay two behind the bridge. This is the last load for that bay. Close it up before leaving."

"Acknowledged," Gavyn said into his comm. He waved at the inspector as they slowly rolled past him with the cargo.

Kash let out another breath.

"Almost there," Gavyn said. "Remember, we are going to help unload it from the forks and place it in the bay."

"Right," Kash responded, his hands sweating even more than usual inside his suit.

"It will be a quick transfer, so don't think, don't question, just move quickly," Gavyn reminded him.

"Got it."

Before he could say more, Kash saw four individuals waving him toward the bay to offload the cargo. He stopped directly in front of them, lowered the lift, and scrambled out of the cab.

Two individuals climbed up the lift and secured cords around the top box. They then lowered it slowly to the ground where Kash, Gavyn, and two other individuals lifted it and placed it into the bay. They did the same thing for the other three boxes until all four were lying side-by-side in the bay.

"This one looks loose," a deep voice said, pointing to the box that held Kash's children. "Pull it open for inspection."

Gavyn placed a firm arm in front of Kash to stop him from jumping forward to stop them. The other five individuals formed a circle around Kash, and together they moved him toward the now open box.

Two people pulled out the items on top of the false bottom exposing the two cryounits. Kash swallowed his outcry. He had to trust Gavyn at this point. He didn't know the entire plan. Then he was being pushed and shoved into the box next to the units.

Gavyn wedged an energy pack just below Kash's right knee. "I see the problem," Gavyn said. "One of these exo suits was caught in the fasteners."

"Got it," someone else said and tore a rip in an exo suit and then threw it to one side. "That one is a loss. Note it on the manifest."

"Noted," another individual responded.

Kash was stuffed awkwardly with one knee wedged into his stomach and the other leg stretched out.

Gavyn grabbed Kash's gloved hand and squeezed. "Good job. I'm looking forward to our next game when this is all over."

"I've already designed my clues," Kash responded, his voice choking back a combination of fear and thankfulness for all Gavyn had done. "This one is a winner. The final answer."

"I'll bet." Gavyn signaled that they needed to put the lid back on and close the forward cargo bay.

Kash heard the lumbering roll of the mechanism as it slipped into the frame and everything went dark. He closed his eyes and tried to regulate his breathing. It was done. Either they survived or they didn't. Whatever happened next was going to depend on the captain. At least they would be away from Ydro-Down. He'd rather be spaced then returned here.

He lifted a gloved hand to the cryounit next to him and rested it on top. He knew Eijaz couldn't feel his touch or was even aware of anything, but Kash felt better for touching the unit. He repeated a childhood prayer in his mind. This had been sung to him as a child every evening on the ship, and again when he and his wife were put into cryosleep.

We seek refuge among the stars.
Our new home calls to us.
May the journey increase our knowledge,
And our spirit respond with wisdom.
It is from the stars we began
and to the stars we will return.
Peace be to us all.

*L*ehana looked throughout Scraff's quarters first thing in the morning for something that would keep the cat alive between exiting the space elevator at the mine and getting into her ship. She'd never seen any environmental suits made for an animal. Now she regretted that she'd never learned about taking live animal cargo while indentured to Hellebor. He'd made offers but she didn't want to worry about becoming attached to anything she had to sell, particularly considering some of the people she sold to.

The cat followed her from room to room as if taking notes to report back to someone. "Come on, beastie," Lehana said. "I promise not to hurt you, just help me out here."

At hearing her voice, the cat rubbed against her leg and weaved in and out almost making her trip.

"Great. That is so helpful right now."

Finally, she came upon the room that was obviously the animal's domain. It contained a variety of padded vessels at different heights, and a box that smelled of feces. Drakh! She'd never thought about how to contain the cat's eliminations.

She couldn't worry about that now. If she didn't find something to secure the cat and keep it safe, she'd have to make a hard decision about killing the thing just so she could take it from Scraff. She had no idea what she was even looking for: a little cat helmet that fit over the head so it could breathe, an incubator of some sort that contained the entire body, or even a cat cryounit would be welcome.

"May I help you, Captain Saar?" a feminine voice said behind her.

Lehana turned quickly. She didn't know anyone else lived with Scraff. The woman was tall and slender. In fact, she was too slender, as if she didn't eat enough. Her face was mottled with what looked like razor cuts that hadn't healed well. It was hard to tell her age with the scarring and the subservient way in which she carried herself. Lehana looked past the scars to meet the woman's gaze.

"And you are?" Lehana asked, putting on her best impression of someone who had the authority and power to ask.

"I am number nine nine nine," she responded. "Maid, cat sitter, concubine, whatever is asked of me by my owner."

Lehana gritted her teeth. This woman was not treated well. All the more reason to take the cat. Perhaps she should take the woman too. Do not care, she scolded herself. You cannot save everyone. You can only save yourself.

"May I help you?" the woman repeated.

"Yes. I've never met a cat before coming to this place." On cue, the cat meowed and settled on Lehana's right foot. "I've wondered how it survived getting here. What kind of transport was used to protect it from the outside."

"You wish to take the cat," the woman said without judgement.

"Oh no," Lehana added with a strained laugh. "Just curious. In case I should ever come across one in the future."

The woman nodded and then walked to a closed cupboard. She opened it to reveal a small incubator. "This allows Layla to breathe," she said. "It also uses a calming agent that puts the cat into a deep sleep so it will not be frightened." Then she pressed a button underneath the unit. It darkened so that no one could see inside. "And that makes sure no one knows you carry a cat off planet, which is illegal on most worlds. It was brought aboard Scraff's cruiser with claims they were baby chicks to be raised for meat exclusively for Scraff's dining pleasure."

Lehana took a deep breath. She was torn as to her next steps. "You seem to know a lot about this. Why is that?"

"I was captured on Raeaa where this cat was raised. I was forced to come with Layla and keep her alive. It was my honor to assure Layla was treated well. However, once off planet, I was enslaved to master Scraff."

Lehana held herself rigid, her hand fisting at one side. Did she dare add to the danger she had already accepted for stealing the cat? She liked revenge like any good pirate, but this was getting more complicated by the minute.

She looked around the room for recording devices or audio monitors.

The woman smiled. "They are disabled. I regularly disable them and add a vid loop so I can go out and come back on my own while the master is gone."

"If you are willing," Lehana began, still unsure if she might be walking into a trap, "I would pay you to help me take this cat to my ship and to stay and care for it. You would be registered as a member of my crew. We would also find other duties for you onboard, for which you would also be paid. And, as a member of my crew, you would share in a percentage of all our profits."

The woman stared without saying anything.

"It's only fair to mention I trade in dangerous places in the Rim. Once you are aboard, there may not be time to let you off before going somewhere most crew would refuse."

"Can't be more dangerous than here," Adira commented.

"It can be. Here you've learned how to stay alive. There have been several times in the Rim when I was sure I'd die. I can't guarantee your safety."

Adira shrugged but made no comment.

"I will not force you to do this, and if you refuse…" She let out a slow breath. May the universe not slap her down for one moment of compassion. "If you refuse, I will not take the cat in order to save you from harm for my actions."

Damn that hurt to say, but even Lehana wouldn't purposefully harm another woman just for her petty revenge for something that happened five turns ago under a different identity. She wasn't Hellebor, no matter how hard he'd tried to make her in his image.

"It is completely your choice," she continued. "I can't promise ease, nor the level of comfort as you may have here." She looked again at the woman. "But, I can promise that no one will touch you without your permission and that you will be treated with dignity and respect while on my ship."

"I agree," the woman said quietly, a tear slipping down to her cheek. "Thank you."

Lehana cleared her throat as if something was caught there. "Now, how will we sneak you and the cat out of here?" She asked.

The woman smiled and tapped her ear comm. "May I speak to master Scraff, please."

Lehana tensed. Was she wrong to trust the woman? It was a trap. Drakh! She wrapped her fingers around the knife inside her vest. If this woman betrayed her, she'd have to kill her. She didn't want to; but she would do it if it meant escaping alive.

"Master," the woman began. "My apologies for interrupting you so early. Captain Saar has requested that I escort her to the ship. She needs assistance with some of her belongings and she is unaccustomed to our protocols for reboarding without you here. May I be allowed to assist in this manner?"

Lehana breathed a little more freely but still didn't let go of the knife in case this was a setup.

"Yes, master. I see the permission and your seal now. I will be ready in your bedroom, as requested, when you return tomor-row. Thank you for this honor." The woman clicked off the link. "No need to be secretive now. His permission and seal have been transferred to the crew chief and the guardians. We will be escorted from here within two kiloseconds. Will you be ready?"

Lehana nodded, and briefly wondered if this was going to be the last time she'd see Ydro-Down or the last contract to trade in Q. Not only was she taking the cat, Scraff's most prized possession, but she was taking his personal slave as well. Perhaps not equally prized by him, but he'd be angry. Very, very angry; and he would certainly report it to Waller.

She might have been able to convince Ming to just give her a slap on the wrist or a fine for taking an animal, but a slave was something else entirely. Taking a slave was punishable by death. Ming would be forced to make her an example to all other traders, no matter what kind of relationship or reputation she'd built with him.

She took in a deep breath and let it out. This wasn't the stupidist thing she'd done by a long shot. The stupidist thing was stealing Hellebor's luxury cruiser. But this was the first time she'd agreed to give up her most lucrative contract to steal a cat and save a slave.

She threw back her head and laughed aloud. It sure made life exciting. After this she'd no longer have Q to trade. She'd find something else for profit. In fact, being as she was screwed, she'd probably keep this load of Q herself. She didn't want to go to Ignis anyway. Now that she'd be marked as a dead woman, what did it matter?

The woman looked at her with concern. "Are you wormy?"

Lehana laughed again, glorying in the challenge. "No. Just coming to grips with a changed lifestyle. No matter." She pointed to the incubator. "What are the chances someone will check the contents?"

"I will provide you with the proper papers for having a rabbit in the incubator," the woman said. "They are approximately the same size and weight, and they are also allowed to be raised for meat for QueCorp executives. In fact, they are sold here at the station."

"You have planned this out," Lehana said with awe in her voice. "You always intended to leave with the cat one day. How? As a stowaway?"

Instead of answering, the woman corralled the cat and placed it into the incubator. It meowed once then curled up and went to sleep. She pressed the button to darken the glass.

"Once this is discovered, they will send trackers," the woman said.

"No worries. I'm one of the best traders in the Rim. We will forego the QueCorp space dock and head to Mùmín within one turn. As Scraff isn't expected back until tomorrow, we'll have a good head start. I'll load a small crew at Mùmín—a medic, a couple push jockeys, and a comms and protocol officer. I'm thinking you'll be billeted as the latter. My AI will put out the call for crew and then put in your name and qualifications for the selection."

"But I don't know anything about comms and protocol," the woman said. "Perhaps you should billet me as cook."

"You know more than you think," Lehana responded with a smile. "Besides I don't trust easily, and right now we are tied together in this. If either of us makes a mistake we both die."

"But—"

"I just watched you get permission to come aboard my ship even though you are a slave. You have already created paperwork for something that doesn't exist, and you are good at subterfuge and planning. Those are all perfect qualifications for a member of my crew. Anything else, Kali can handle until you are trained. I've flown this ship on my own many times."

"I owe you my life, the woman said, her voice filled with hope and confidence. "You will not regret this."

Lehana chuckled. "Oh, I already regret it, but it's too late now." She paused. "One more thing before we take those steps out the door. I need a name for the crew manifest. Nine Nine Nine will definitely not work for me. What name would you prefer?"

"My own," she responded. "Adira Baumann."

"Is that name known by anyone at QueCorp?" Lehana asked. "If it is, you need to choose another.."

"No," Adira responded. "I was sold to Scraff as a number so that my family would not know what happened to me. By now, if they are still alive, they would believe I am dead."

Lehana nodded and keyed the name Adira Baumann into an

encrypted message to Kali, along with the details of her billet and a berth assignment near the bridge.

"Done," Lehana said when she received confirmation back from her AI. She held her p-tab unit out to Adira. "You need to acknowledge the usual crew contract. Nothing is owed to any heirs if you die on my ship. Anything you learn from me or about me is confidential. If I discover you released information without my permission the penalty is banishment to a planet in the dead zone."

Adira nodded and used her finger to scrawl her name. "No fingerprint or eye scan?" she asked.

"I don't do that," Lehana said. "I don't care about your past and I don't want anyone monitoring crew assignments on Mùmín to care or check either. I also don't want any bureaucracy connecting you to a stolen slave from Ydro-Down. Can you be ready with the cat and anything else you need within half a kilosecond?"

"Easily," Adira answered. "I've been planning this for eleven turns."

Lehana smiled and waited for the guardians to come escort them to her ship. She knew what it felt like to be taken from everything she knew, knowing she'd never see family or friends again. She did not know what it was like to be a slave. At least with Hellebor he was fair—not easy, not forgiving, but fair in the end. As a slave, there was no fairness. In fact, there was no recognition that you were human.

She'd wanted to say that Adira would be family now, but she couldn't. That assumed too much of a connection, and Lehana could not afford connections—ever. It was best that Adira stayed independent and trusted no one. That was the only way to survive in the Rim, and Lehana would never take that freedom away from her.

THOUGH EXHAUSTED, Gavyn opened the game and began to play instead of falling directly to sleep. He'd worked through last night and this morning, an eighteen-hour shift making sure everything was secure. He was too tired to sleep and the game might calm him.

They'd set it up so it would look like Kash was on the other end. He'd done all he could to get Kash and his children off Ydro-Down. The ship had been picked up as scheduled and moved to the catapult. It was cradled in the accelerator now and scheduled to launch early in the morning.

Sometime tomorrow afternoon it would be obvious that Kash was not on shift and that his children were gone as well. There would be repercussions. They'd all be docked pay. Whenever a miner went missing it was assumed all were responsible. There would be an investigation and someone would be blamed, whether they were part of it or not. Someone always had to be blamed.

It was likely someone would be killed and held up as an example. Gavyn sighed. He'd long ago made peace that when the rebellion started there would be collateral damage. Was it worth one individual's life to give three individuals a chance at freedom? He'd never know for sure. Because he might never know whether Kash and his children survived and found freedom.

How did anyone measure the worth of one life against another?

One thing Gavyn knew for sure. It was unlikely Kash would ever be found and brought back as an example of a failed escape. That meant that in every miner's mind he had made it off planet, and that gave them hope.

Hope was insidious. It clung in the crevices and hidden pockets of the heart and mind. It found purchase in the most unlikely of places and it abided with patience, waiting like a vampire that delivered a single deadly bite and then retreated, changing that one life forever. Every strike against QueCorp, no matter how small would reinforce that hope. Over time, that hope would grow until the majority were ready to risk their lives for freedom.

In one of their first games, after Kash had learned the coding framework, Gavyn had asked him: What are you willing to risk for freedom?

Kash hadn't responded then. He didn't know then that his hope could be realized. But this evening, Kash had said his clues held the answer.

Gavyn worked through the clues quickly. Kash had made it easy, choosing shorter words as the answers. Gavyn put them in numbered order: rise, fears, heart, right, everything. He wasn't sure if his interpretation or sequencing was exactly what Kash would say, but he could feel the essence was there.

Freedom allows me to rise above my fears to do what I know is right. For that I must risk everything.

Gavyn smiled as he shut down the game and crawled into his cot. He'd found a true believer in Kash. An idealist to the core. No matter the end Kash and his children might find, it was in the act of trying for a better life that Kash had already found freedom.

May we all be as fortunate.

CHAPTER 7

$\mathcal{L}$ ehana paced on the bridge. She'd always hated waiting for launch. But today was even worse as she was harboring a stolen cat and Adira. Not that she believed anyone would attempt to board the ship while they were in the catapult. Everything was secured and they'd have to move her ship off the catapult to board it, costing millions of DICs in lost time and screwing the schedule for loads behind her. Still, she needed every advantage of time once launched to make sure no one followed. Once Scraff realized Adira and the cat were gone he'd certainly get Ming to send someone to find them.

The cargo section of her ship had already successfully launched and was in orbit around Ydro-Down. Once the bridge and crew section of the *Phoenix* launched, they'd have to match speed and trajectory to pick up the orbiting cargo before leaving this sector. That was the part that worried Lehana. How long would it take them to hook up? What time would Scraff arrive? Would they get away in time?

She cracked her knuckles and paced again. They'd been

sitting in this catapult for five hours and she was close to losing her cool.

A roar of machinery echoed through the ship and Lehana pumped her fist as she scrambled into her captains chair. She finished securing her safety harness, then said to the AI, "Inform Adira to strap herself and the cat in securely. It's going to be a ride."

"Catapult push in five...four...three...two...one."

The ship's initial acceleration and G force was constant for the first one thousand kilometers, but Lehana knew that was going to change in a few minutes.

"Laser infusion in five...four...three...two...one."

When the lasers hit, the entire ship shuddered like a space elevator tether in an earthquake. A deep rumble shook the cabin as the *Phoenix'* mass driver reflected the energy push from the catapult to drive the ship up a steep incline and out of Ydro-Down's gravity well. Lehana was thrown back against her seat as they accelerated at three Gs. It felt like a jellicant was sitting on her chest. Finally, the ship ripped through the thin atmosphere with a momentary flash of light and the engine throttled down to reduce the stress on the structure.

Just one more minute, Lehana thought to herself, struggling to breathe normally.

At main engine cut-off, thrust dropped to zero in just a half-second, the pressure on her body vanished, and she was afloat under her harness. She choked back the automatic response to empty her stomach that always happened when she first entered zero G.

"Time to dock with cargo?" Lehana asked the AI as she swallowed hard.

"Twenty-three minutes," Kali responded.

Lehana blew out a lot of air, as she released her harness and floated horizontal with one hand grasping the arm of her chair. "Any messages? Any trackers?"

"None yet. Should I extend my sensors?"

"Monitor Ydro-Down traffic both at the station and at the elevator. If they wanted to send someone after us, it would be a high speed cruiser."

"Monitoring now."

Lehana traveled hand over hand from one grip to another to get to her environmental suit in the far corner of the bridge. Once there she floated above it and then slid into the suit from the top. Clamped against the wall she was able to use her hands to adjust the fit.

"Inform Adira that she and the cat are to remain in the shielded quarters until we dock at Mùmín. Just in case anyone is scanning and counting life signs, I don't want her found."

"Message sent," Kali confirmed. "Seven minutes to cargo coupling."

Lehana pulled down the helmet and attached it to her suit. "Release suit restraints."

When she felt the weightlessness again, she pushed off from the wall to propel herself to the rear of the ship where the cargo would be again attached to the *Phoenix*. Though Ydro-Down push jockeys would be guiding it in, she wanted to be ready in case something went wrong. She also wanted to inspect the coupling before they took off.

She stepped into the airlock, the door sealing behind her, and walked across to the outer bay door. She attached her tether near the large door at the other side. With twelve meters of open space about to greet her, she definitely wanted to be secured. She might be greeted by calm vacuum, or there might be debris or docking tethers flying at her. Within a minute she saw the push jockey in the window. She gave him a thumbs up and opened the outer door.

The giant cargo section was only a couple hundred meters behind them. The push jockeys already had it linked with tethers to a tow ship. The only thing left was to maneuver it to the coupling mechanism without bumping into the bridge and crew quarters with more than a slight movement.

Kali began speaking in her ear. "Coupling in thirty…twenty-nine…twenty-eight…"

Lehana couldn't help but hold her breath. She'd only done this once before, when she'd first bought the *Phoenix* and the cargo section separately. That was more than twenty yearunits ago. Since then, all their port calls had been at space stations able to accommodate them.

"Ten…nine…eight…" Kali's count continued in her ear.

The cargo section looked very large now, as if it would try to squeeze into the airlock.

"Three…two…one…contact."

The ship jolted slightly and Lehana side stepped a couple times before regaining her balance.

"Securing couple," Kali announced.

Two push jockeys floated to the doorway and looked down at the coupling, and then nodded. One gestured to Lehana to inspect it as well. She floated out the door and worked her way down to the large connection. After inspecting each side and underneath she nodded her approval. One of the jockeys gave her a thumbs up and then the tethers released from the cargo bay. The six jockeys floated up with the tethers and moved on to the tow vehicle.

Lehana finally let out her breath and took her place in the airlock, closing the door. When it equalized she moved to the other door and exited before removing her helmet.

"Scan cargo," she said as she propelled herself back to the bridge. "Any damage?"

"No damage," Kali verified.

"Thank the stars." Lehana shimmied out of the environmental suit and took her place back at the captain's chair. "Add gravity at one half G," she instructed. "Let's get out of this orbit and on to Mùmín Station as quickly as possible."

Immediately, she felt the comfort of being able to feel firmly attached to the ship again. It took another few minutes for her body to readjust too.

"Time to Mùmín station?"

"Five hours, twenty-nine minutes."

Lehana stretched and rolled her head around her shoulders to get out the stiffness. "Put out the message I'm looking for crew." She looked at the notes she'd dictated into her p-tab. "Medic, navigator, two push jockeys, and a protocol comms officer. Use the job descriptions and contracts we've used in the past."

"Done," Kalli responded within seconds. "An application and accepted contract for the protcol comms position has already been received from an Adira Baumann."

Lehana smiled. She loved it when a plan came together.

Over the next five hours, Lehana sorted through crew applications as they came in. Anyone living on space dock looking for work knew to get in fast or lose a position. Five hours later she'd selected the three new crew members and had Kali transmit the selections to space dock, get signed contracts and ask them to be ready to board as soon as they were assigned a dock location.

Fortunately, with a large ship and no need to load cargo, they would be placed at the outer rim of the station. That suited Lehana just fine. She wanted to get in and out as fast as she could get crew onboard. By now, Scraff had surely informed authorities of his missing cat and slave. Though they had a good headstart on any trackers, she didn't want the space dock nickers chasing her down or boarding her ship to look for an escaped slave.

"Slot accepted," Kali said to the AI assigning space dock. "Last one on the ring," she added to Lehana.

"Perfect. Alert the selected crew to meet us at that location in fifteen." Lehana headed for the docking door. "I want them on the ramp, ready to go. Don't shut the engines completely down in case we need to move out fast."

On her way, she stopped at Adira's cabin and rang for entry. "Time to take your place at comms," Lehana said.

Adira poked her head out the door and looked both ways before coming out and closing the door behind her.

Lehana barely recognized her. She'd changed from long blonde tresses and an obedient child-like appearance to a woman who clearly shouted confidence. Her now ebony hair, with blue and purple streaks, was cut short on both sides of her head with a mohawk on top. A hard face covering, forming a partial mask, in dark blue with neon purple starbursts started at her scalp on the left side and worked its way down her face to her neck in a pattern that covered her scars. Dressed in the usual crew skinsuit, she'd already attached the comms leads to her forehead and chest.

"Too much?" Adira asked, her mouth curving into a big smile.

"A good look for someone saying: mess with me at your peril."

"Exactly my purpose," Adira said.

"Head to the bridge and monitor comms. We've passed the time you were probably missed, so I do expect Mùmín nickers to be traveling to us at the same time as the crew. We need to get crew on and leave before the nickers get to us."

"I'll do what I can to make them have all the right paper-work before boarding," Adira said. "That usually does the trick."

Lehana nodded and walked away. Adira was definitely the right person for the comms job. She obvoiusly had a lot of experience covering Scraff's backside.

When she reached the dock door, Lehana took a big breath. "Status?" she asked before opening the door.

"Three crew in line to board. No nickers in sight."

Lehana blew out her breath. "Let's get this done." She pushed the button and the door opened. "Papers and identifica-tion," she said to the three individuals waiting on the other side.

"Medic," the first person said, her voice like a soothing mist as she handed over her identity card for scanning. "Stambuli Etienam."

Lehana had to look up at least two head heights to see her face. Tall and strong, the woman wore a neck-to-knee white tunic that was form-fitted on the front, but billowed into a butterfly shape on the back that also draped her dark arms above the elbow. The bright white contrasted beautifully with her smooth ebony skin giving her an almost angelic glow. On her left arm was the required large metal bracelet of the medic that contained a touch screen link to the Rim library of medi-cine. White leggings appeared beneath the hem of the tunic to completely cover her feet in a soft-shaped boot.

Even the self-propelled luggage was encased in white. White was the traditional color of medics, but Lehana had not seen one that embraced white for everything to this degree.

"Welcome aboard. You will find the medical bay to your left approximately ten meters down the hall."

A man and woman stepped forward next. Both wore identical outfits of multi-belted brown jackets with tool packs at chest level and hip level. Beneath the jacket were loose fitting skirts and heavy duty boots.

"Push jockeys," they both said together. "Twins."

"Erik," one said.

"Kire," the other echoed.

"Thomas," they both said together.

Lehana smiled. She'd never employed twins. She could see how working in the vac together could be enhanced. "Welcome aboard. Your quarters are side by side twenty meters to the left, just past the medical bay."

Erik fell behind Kire as they entered the ship and executed a military left turn together before heading down the hall.

"There's a problem," Adira said into Lehana's comms. "We need to lock down now before we are boarded."

"Close dock door," Lehana said to Kali. "Secure ship for takeoff."

As she walked back to the bridge she tapped into Adira's comms.

"No, there is no one aboard other than the four crew recently loaded," Adira stated in a professional and calm voice.

The florid face of the police comms officer filled the screen. "Mr. Scraff reports one personal slave and one cat missing from his quarters at Ydro-Down. In addition, a miner and two children in cryosleep are also missing. Request permission to search the ship."

"One moment," Adira responded. "I will inform the captain."

"Impulse power to leave dock," Lehana said. "Are we free of the locks?"

"Locks disengaged," Kali reported. "Impulse power engaged."

"All crew secure your position," Lehana announced into the ship's com. "We may be leaving in a hurry."

"We request you not leave space dock," the police comms repeated twice.

"We have an urgent delivery," Adira said, again as if this was nothing abnormal. "Without the appropriate paperwork for a search, we must leave."

"The paperwork is on its way." The police comms speaker sounded a bit agitated. "An honest captain would allow us to search."

Lehana laughed at that. She'd never been an honest captain and she wasn't starting now.

"Clearing space dock," Kali said. "Turning one-hundred-eighty degrees, engines ready for ignition."

"Continue with impulse power until we are far enough to engage without burning the end of the station," Lehana said. "Float out as if we have nothing to hide."

"Return to space dock," the police comms demanded.

"No more engagement," Lehana instructed Adira.

"Captain Saar," police comms said. "I have properly executed paperwork from Ming Waller at Ydro-Down to search the ship for four slaves and a cat. Return to space dock at once."

"Keep moving, slowly" Lehana said evenly. "I hope you've resolved the Q insertion problem."

"A virus was spotted and removed," Kali confirmed.

"Scan for the best place to open a wormhole within a half gigameter."

"Scanning," Kali replied.

"Give me comms," Lehana said.

Adira patched her directly to the Mùmín station police.

"This is Captain Saar speaking, I have no slaves. I have only the crew I boarded. Check your records. You had every application, every approval, and checked each person yourself before boarding."

"Yes, but we did not search your ship," the officer replied. "We now have justification to search your ship."

"Good opening for wormhole within point three eight gigameter," Kali said.

"Prepare for acceleration to wormhole point," Lehana said, as she secured her own harness.

"We are revved for qubition injection," Lehana continued with Mùmín Station police. "We've been contracted by QueCorp to deliver cargo to the other side of the galaxy. Check the registered paperwork. Please relay to Mr. Waller that I promise I will do a thorough search of my ship when I have completed my contracted delivery. Naturally, if I find any stowaway slaves they will be returned to Ydro-Down as soon as possible."

Lehana placed dark goggles over her eyes, reclined her seat backward at a forty-five degree angle and said, "Light her up!"

The ship accelerated, pushing her and Adira back into their seats. "If you haven't traversed a wormhole before, or hate the pain and feelings of disorientation," Lehana said to the crew in a ship-wide announcement. "I suggest you take the knockout drug in your personal med kit now. I will not tolerate any wormy crew members. Your choice."

The Gs built quickly from one to three, the heavy weight pinning her to her seat as they approached the injection point.

"Where are we going?" Adira asked Lehana, her breathing labored.

"Kollaiyar, if the wormhole remains stable."

"See you on the other side," Adira said as she pressed the injector against her skin and fell asleep in her harness within seconds.

"Injecting qubition," Kali announced.

"Let's not piss in the vac again," Lehana said, under her

breath. Certainly they wouldn't have two horrific wormhole traverses in the same year.

Lehana knew it was best not to watch what was going on, but she was too much of a control-freak to completely trust the AI to get them out of trouble. She steeled herself to the upside down and inside out views that would occur.

The *Phoenix* began its free-fall through the outer horizon of the stabilized hole. It felt as if her body was being stretched taut, her feet rushing toward the center of the hole. The building G force on her chest, four...five...six Gs echoed what her eyes saw, her body being stretched beyond belief. If there weren't real pain she'd be terrified at seeing her legs look like they were several kilometers long. Just as she thought the pain was more than she could bear, the ship counteracted that pull of gravity and she could briefly breathe again.

A sudden flash of seemingly infinite light briefly etched an image of the entire history of the universe in her mind. Before she could process that image, everything around her began to warp, like she was entering a large fish-eye lens. The image of the other side of the hole appeared and expanded around her, swallowing her up.

Lehana knew better than to look left or right. She closed her eyes for a moment. She had looked around her first time through a wormhole and almost lost it. As they crossed the black ring to the other side, she could see the back of her own head as the flow of space turned around. It was something her brain just couldn't process.

Now, instead of being pulled inward, the ship was being pushed outward. She gritted her teeth while the ship once again had to compensate for the change in gravitational pull. She again felt pressure and stretching of her bones. Her body now being pulled in the opposite direction than before. When the pressure lessened she opened her eyes and took a deep breath. Another quick flash of light, this time containing an instant image of the entire future of the universe. As her eyes readjusted, the *Phoenix* was spit out of the wormhole like an unwanted seed pip. virus.

Millions of twinkling lights in the dark sky greeted her. Calm, barely moving as the ship's speed decelerated to sub5 breaking toward their destination.

Lehana welcomed the calm of a normal starfield—no more warping, no more stretching. She took several deep breaths to calm her racing heart. If she didn't know better she'd think everything that just happened was her imagination. Though humanity had found a way to traverse wormholes, it would never be normal and she would never get used to it.

"Time to location?" she finally managed to ask, her throat parched from the pain of the traverse.

"Nine hours, seventeen minutes, and forty three seconds," Kali responded.

"Good. Time to prepare." Lehana turned to Adira who seemed not at all fatigued from the transit. "Send a message to Kollaiyar station that we will be taking our shuttle to the surface to purchase goods."

"They will ask for the identity of the two people," Adira reminded her.

"You and me." Lehana said. "I need to unload at least half of this Q at deep discount, just in case we need to disappear for a while. While I'm looking for people who want to buy, you can go food shopping."

Adira's eyes widened. "Food? Like the real kind?" She moved from side to side like a giddy teenager. "I haven't had anything except nutrition tablets since Scraff took me from Raeaa."

"I'm sure Scraff wasn't living off nutrition tablets," Lehana said. The corner of her mouth tightened on one side.

"No," Adira agreed, her head lowered. "I don't remember him ever having a nutritional tablet. Of course, I cooked for him and had a taste or two to test the flavor. But whenever I cooked he watched me to make sure I didn't get any type of a meal out of it. Less for him that way."

Lehana shook her head. Once again, she was sorry she hadn't killed him all those years ago. Maybe that would have saved Adira from all the pain and indignity she'd suffered over the years as his slave.

Adira brightened and forced a smile. "But on Raeaa we had real food every day, one of the advantages of being a farming community with land to grow fruits and vegetables and other plants."

"We will try to avoid nutritional tablets as meals here as much as we can," Lehana said. "I'll transfer one million DICs to your personal account. Get whatever you want. Just remember you are buying for the entire crew and it needs to last a minimum of thirty days." She took a deep breath and wondered once again how Adira had borne the weight of Scraff's indignities for all this time. Lehana was pretty sure she would have killed him after or during the first forced rape.

"Any specific requests?" Adira asked, taking her out of her murderous thoughts.

Lehana licked her lips. "Pasta with tomato sauce and something resembling cheese. It's been at least two turns since I've had any kind of pasta. "

"Meat-equivalent?" Adira asked.

"If you can find some of that soy-based protein with the right amount of spices and vegetables to actually taste like beef or pork, I'd be in food ecstasy for days. In fact, if you can find that, get at least ten days of servings for everyone. A well-fed crew is a loyal crew."

"And I can cook for everyone," Adira suggested.

"No need to do that. You have an important position already. Everyone can cook for themselves. You are not a slave here."

"But I enjoy it," Adira said. "If I'm cooking for myself, it isn't that much more trouble to make enough for five." She paused and looked Lehana straight in the eye. "Please. I…need to feel useful. I need to feel that I'm pulling my weight. That I'm not just a charity case."

"You are not a charity case," Lehana said, her voice commanding. "You have good skills, and you already gave me a huge gift."

"I've given you no gifts," Adira said.

"The truth is taking you from Scraff was a gift to me."

"I don't understand."

"Scraff tried to rape me many turns ago."

Adira gasped.

"He didn't get away with it, but he tried. When I didn't agree he tried to choke me. I stabbed him good and ran. I wish I'd killed him."

Adira's eyes were wide and her breathing audible.

"When I realized it was Scraff I was meeting on Ydro-Down all I could think of was what was the most precious thing I could take from him."

"The cat," Adira said, full realization in her voice.

"Exactly," Lehana confirmed. "And you."

"He would not value me as much as the cat. He has the power to find another slave and concubine whenever he wants. But I am grateful you saw value in me."

"Both you and the cat got me my revenge. That is a satisfactory trade." Lehana bit her lower lip, then turned away, clearing her throat. "Kali, is the rest of the crew recovered from the wormhole yet?"

"Yes, all are awake and in their rooms."

"Good. Ask them to assemble on the bridge in two hours for assigned duties while we are docked at Kollaiyar station."

CHAPTER 8

Kash groaned and tried to turn from his back to his side within the storage compartment he shared with his children. It had been a tough wormhole transit without padding. He could feel the swelling on one side of his head, as well as both his shoulders and hips from being banged against the edge of the box on one side and Z-Huang's cryopod on the other.

He remembered the displays of the past and future universe with each light emission. Though he knew of that phenomenon, he'd never experienced it himself and he didn't think the light would come through the storage compartment where he hid. In that moment, he had feared the cargo compartment had been separated from the ship and he would be dead soon. Then it was over and he was again confined in the cargo apartment but battered.

Once on his side, he placed a hand across the smaller pod and pulled up to peer at the status display.

His breath caught. A red distress light was blinking.

"No. No, no, no." He tapped it to see if it was a momentary glitch.

The display read: Status critical. Oxygen depletion in thirty-eight minutes.

He squished his torso between the top of the unit to see if Eijaz' unit was undamaged.

"No!"

It read exactly the same.

He tried to lift the lid of the cargo pod to get out, but it wouldn't budge.

Running fingers all around the edge, he searched for a release.

None!

When they'd placed the cryounits inside and Kash had crawled in, Gavyn had made a point that it was unlocked so they could get out whenever the opportunity presented itself. But now he was clearly stuck without any ability to get help for his children.

He lifted his legs and banged as hard as he could trying to break open the lid. Nothing. He tried again. There was no way he was going to let his children die now. Not after everyone had sacrificed to get them off Ydro-Down.

He banged with both feet once more again and again and yelled as loud as he could. "Get me out. Get me out."

"Opening cargo," a gruff male voice said above him. "Do not move until instructed. Weapons are set to kill."

"I'm unarmed," Kash said. "My children are in distress. Please, just help them."

"Children?" a compassionate voice asked. "What kind of a stupid parent would stowaway with children on a freighter?"

Kash heard scraping, as if a lock was stuck and being manually removed.

"When the lid is lifted, do not move," the gruff voice repeated. "You will be killed."

The lid lifted and Kash didn't even breathe.

A tall woman in all white peered inside. "Children in cryo. Red alarms. Move them to the med bay. I'll need to tend to them and make sure they don't come out of cryo too quickly." She looked at Kash. "How long have they been in cryo?"

He had to calculate backward from the time his wife died until now.

"How long?" she demanded.

"Seven and a half yearunits," Kash finally said. Yes, he was pretty sure that was it. "Give or take a quarter turn," he added. "Please. Please save them. They are innocents."

The tall medic and another woman—one who had nearly half her face obscured with a decorative metal plate—took the two cryounits and left.

"Come out slowly," the man with the weapon pointed at him instructed.

It took three tries for Kash to stand, his balance still off, and the adrenaline for saving his children now expended. Once standing he looked beyond the man with the gun and recognized the captain. The woman who had responded, unknowingly, to his cryoborn star connection. He sagged against the wall.

"Stow your weapons," the captain instructed. "He can barely stand. How is he going to hurt us?"

This was not exactly how he'd planned to formally introduce himself to the captain and put forward the plight of his children.

"Thank you," Kash said. "My children? Please, Captain, may I be with them. You can search me. You can strip me if you want, hand cuff me in the med bay, put a guard on me. I'll do anything you ask, just let me be with them when they come out of cryo. If your sentence is death, I only ask you give me time with them."

"By your clothing, you must be the miner I'm accused of stealing," the captain said. "If so, you have no reason to expect any favors from me. You've cost me a hundred million DICs and I'll never trade in Q again."

Kash sank to the floor. How could it be that everything he'd dreamed was now in jeopardy? Would he have been better off staying on Ydro-Down, biding his time as he had since his wife's death?

The gruff man pulled him up to stand again. "Captain Saar is talking to you. She has spared your life. For now. The least you can do is stand."

Kash nodded and once more braced himself against the wall.

"Drakh!" Captain Saar said. "It's not very satisfying beating a man who's already down." She paced in front of him, then suddenly threw back her head and laughed like he'd seen her do when he discovered her on the bridge in the mine. "A half-dead miner and two cryo children. They said four slaves were stolen. Four! They count those two cryo children as slaves too? Damn bureaucrats."

"Four?" Kash dared to ask. "We are only three. I promise I did not stowaway with a fourth."

"I know where the fourth is." She blew out a big breath. "Drakh! Me. An idealistic slave stealer. That's rich."

She turned to the man who stood closest to Kash. "Lock him in an empty crew's quarters. I'll have Kali lock down the access to any comms or computing on the ship. Get him a clean set of clothes." She turned back to Kash. "Take a shower and then ping Erik to escort you to the med bay."

"Are you sure, Captain?" Erik asked. "We know nothing about him. For all we know, he could be a saboteur."

"Do you know saboteurs who travel with two cryo children?"

Erik shook his head.

"Of course not. He's a man escaping the planet with his two children. I can't think of a single reason someone would risk the lives of his children on an unknown freighter unless he was desperate."

"But—" Erik said.

"I don't have time to deal with this right now," the captain shouted and pointed at him. "Then I'll decide what's going to happen to him later."

"Yes, Captain," Erik responded. "Shall I secure the prisoner when I come to attend the meeting?"

The captain stared at Kash in such a way that he felt uncomfortable. It was as if she was stripping him with a painful whip.

"Stambuli will want to stay with the two scrubbies. Remind her to have a good tranquilizer on hand in case she needs to use it. When you leave, secure the med bay so that no one can exit."

"I wouldn't hurt the medic tending my children," Kash said quietly.

The captain turned back to him again, one eyebrow quirked upward and her head tilted. "Wouldn't you?"

He was taken aback by the way in which she asked the question, as if she truly cared what the answer might be. Was it possible this seemingly hard-edged woman had a softer side? He wouldn't mind finding out for himself.

He swallowed then shook his head slowly. He still missed his wife.

He looked her straight in the eye. "I am not that kind of man."

"Hmmm," she said, her index finger tapping her lips. "I wonder."

Then the captain turned on her heel and strode away without a backward look. Each step echoed in Kash's head.

"DRAKH! DRAKH! DRAKH!" Lehana strode back to the bridge, putting as much distance between herself and that damn stowaway—with two kids in tow. She should have suspected a stowaway when she got the message she was being charged with four slaves. She just didn't take the time to think. She was in a hurry to get off planet, all for revenge on a man who had no idea who she really was. Hellebor had always told her that vengeance would get her killed one day.

"Any tails?" Lehana said aloud. Certainly by now someone had been asked to find her and bring back the stolen slaves.

"Nothing on the scan," Kali responded.

"What is the range?" Lehana asked.

"The entire distance between where we left the wormhole and our current location. If someone followed us into the wormhole the scan would alert."

Lehana let out a breath. No one followed them in. She knew that. Kali would have alerted her. Now she only had to worry about someone taking the contract who plied their trade in this quadrant.

Maybe they shouldn't stop at Kollaiyar. A place where many pirates and smugglers congregated to make trades was also a place where vac trackers took on contracts. Vac trackers, like assassins, rarely met their contractors face to face, preferring to make all deals virtually. It might be that her image had already been transmitted to several potential trackers.

"Any noise about vac tracker contracts?" Lehana asked. She'd done vac tracking on occasion herself when she was with Hellebor. But it wasn't something she enjoyed. Too much subterfuge and she always wanted to look a contractor in the eye before taking a job.

Two shakes later, Kali answered. "None on the usual places. But my information doesn't include the private single-sourced contractors."

"Right," Lehana sighed. That was her biggest fear. With QueCorp's power and contacts, they likely had several single-sourced vac trackers already on their list.

"Course change?" Kali asked.

"No," Lehana said after a long pause. "We'll just need to get in and out of Kollaiyar fast. Engage protocols for ship identity change."

"We haven't used the *Mary Bowser* for eight turns," Kali suggested.

Lehana chuckled. Kali loved to pick ship identities based on ancient earth history. "That will do."

"Shall we park the cargo somewhere before we get to Kollaiyar?"

"Yes. Any nice asteroid fields in the area?" Lehana asked.

"None in our direct line. One moment."

"Call Adira to the bridge. I need her to transmit our change of plan to Kollaiyar Station."

"Calling. Adira is on her way. I've identified the second moon of Bhugarbha as an appropriate choice," Kali said. "Both the moon, Nedra, and the planet are uninhabited and have no useful minerals for mining. High mountains on the moon surround a valley that would be secretive. Nedra gravity one tenth sol norm making it fairly easy to lift again with the shuttle driver. We will time release and cargo contact on the dark side when we enter orbit."

"Will we need to tether the cargo bay to the planet?" Lehana asked.

"That would be the wisest choice."

"Alert Erik and Kire they will be needed for that."

Adira appeared at Lehana's side.

"Captain? Problem?" Adira asked as she entered the bridge and moved to Lehana's right.

"I need you to send a message to Kollaiyar station. Tell them the *Phoenix* is changing course and will not be stopping there. Cancel the shuttle we scheduled."

"But...I don't understand. The supplies? The..."

"Food?" Lehana smiled knowing how much that would mean to her.

Adira nodded.

"We will be stopping but under a different name, and you and I will also have different names. By now, if any trackers have been given our ship information, they will be waiting at our next scheduled stop."

"Of course," Adira acknowledged. "And where is the *Phoenix's* next stop?"

"Ignis, of course," Lehana answered. "QueCorp did contract us to deliver the Q load to that star-forsaken planet. It is so close to the edge of the dead zone that no one dares deliver there."

"Except you," Adira acknowledged.

"Only once before. A long time ago."

Lehana paused as she remembered Hellebor taking her there to teach her a lesson about the results of seeking revenge. It was the last planet that still had a full military contingent directly descended from those who waged the Oblivion War. They still tried to get qubition. They still wanted to make q-bombs in secret and use them as a lever to take back power and re-establish law and order in the Rim. They offered billions of credits to QueCorp to get it to them. But no one would agree to deliver to them, even Hellebor who didn't seem to have any morale scruples.

"I swore nothing would make me go back there. For two years I said no to QueCorp," Lehana continued.

"Yet you accepted their contract."

"I would have agreed to sleep with the devil himself on Ignis," Lehana said, "if it helped me get off Ydro-Down."

"Would you have carried through with it?"

Lehana took in a deep breath and let it out slowly. "I don't know," she answered honestly. "And I'll never know. Once I made the decision to take the cat and help you, I knew there was no reason to risk my life going there when the sentence for harboring a slave is death. But Ming doesn't know that."

Adira shook her head. "He is certainly aware that you know the sentence is death."

Lehana chuckled. "Yes, but my reputation precedes me. He also knows I always have a plan. No matter the danger I have a backup plan. I hope he believes that I would still go to Ignis. In fact, I hope that he believes I will call him with proof of delivery and wait an entire turn somewhere for him to transfer the one hundred million DIC bonus, while he's passing my location to a vac tracker."

"And he would expect that you have a backup plan," Adira finished for her, "But his own hubris would make him believe he can catch you."

"Exactly. But even I'm not that greedy. Nor that stupid."

"Let's hope he is," Adira said.

"Revenge is a powerful motivator," Lehana said.

Adira nodded, but said nothing.

Lehana watched her as she turned to the comms panel and connected to Kollaiyar station, providing them with the *Phoenix'* changed routing. "Station acknowledges change and hopes to see us on our return from Ignis."

"Time to moon intersection?" Lehana asked Kali.

"Ten shakes until Nedra orbit acquired."

Lehana thumbed her comms unit. "Kire. Erik. Bridge meeting cancelled. You have less than ten minutes to suit up. We will be dropping cargo on Nedra, second moon of Bhugarbha. I need you to ride it down, secure it, and stay there until we return from Kollaiyar."

"What the freeze?" Erik responded. "What am I to do with our miner and his scrubbies?"

"I'll take care of him," Lehana said. "You better move it or Kire's going alone."

"Drakh! Two days out and she's already expecting the impossible."

Lehana could hear him breathing hard as he moved quickly to his quarters to get into his exo suit.

"Estimated time of pod habitation on Nedra?" Kire asked.

"Less than a half day on Kollaiyar. You will each receive a two million DIC bonus for hazard pay on this one."

"Thank you," Kire said.

"At least that's something," Erik acknowledged. "And if you don't come back from Kollaiyar?"

"That's the hazard pay," Lehana said. "Pod has five days of supplies, but you won't need them. We'll be back. You can count on it."

"One full day is all I'm giving you," Erik said.

Now in his exo suit, Lehana tracked him on her viewscreen as he moved quickly down the corridor toward the cargo bay.

"If you haven't picked us up by start of next day on Kollai-yar," Erik continued, his breathing slightly labored, "I'm putting out a call for bidders and offering the entire Q load at discount prices."

Lehana laughed. "You do that, Erik. You'll probably die in the crossfire of people fighting to get to you first. I'll be back. You know my reputation. I always keep my promises."

"Yes, you do," Kire confirmed. "I have Erik now. We have secured the airlock and pushed off to the pod where we will tether."

"Good." Lehana turned on the aft viewscreen to watch them. "Time to moon orbit?" she asked Kali.

"Two minutes to acquire Nedra orbit."

Their tethers now secured to the center of the aft cargo bay, the two push jockeys propelled themselves toward the cargo bay doors. Both stopped at the same time on either side of the doors, their hands on a metal hold.

"Open cargo bay doors,"Erik instructed.

"Doors opening now," Kali said.

Looking like a synchronized dance team in slow motion, the two climbed outside the door and reached below them to remove the locking mechanism that secured the cargo bay to the ship.

"Unlocking cargo holds," Erik and Kire said at the same time. Then a moment later echoed together, "Holds unlocked."

"The beauty of twin push jockeys," Lehana acknowledged as she watched them work at opposite ends of the bay. It was as if they shared one brain.

"Orbit acquired," Kali informed everyone.

"Activate tether tow." Again Kire and Erik spoke at the same time as the tethers pulled them back to the pod.

"Unlock pod door," Kire said.

"Opening pod door," Kali confirmed.

The pod door sprang open on one side and interior lights illuminated the thirty-eight square meter pod.

"Angled for cargo release to Nedra's no-return valley, " Kali spoke again.

"Acknowledged," Lehana said.

"Don't like that valley name," Erik complained.

"Kali's trying to make a joke," Lehana said. "Some new algorithm she's been testing to sound more friendly."

"Not funny, Kali," Erik said. "Keep jokes to yourself."

"Ignore her. Nothing is named on this moon. It's useless for colony habitation or commercial use. No one has bothered with claiming it or naming anything."

Kire placed one hand inside the pod and then released the tether from her waist. She pulled herself inside first. Erik followed the same procedure and was beside Kire within a few moments.

"Close pod door," Kire requested.

Kali sent the signal and the door shut securely.

"Ten seconds to cargo bay release,"Kali announced. "Ten… nine…eight…"

"Take care of that Q, while you're enjoying your stay on Nedra," Lehana said. "We'll be back soon and you'll love the real food you will dine on tonight."

"Three…two…one…release." Kali finished.

The entire cargo section floated away from the bridge and crew quarters. The ship moved several kilometers away before firing a small burst. Lehana watched as Kire and Erik steered the Q load toward the moon's valley. The twins were good. They'd both worked on space docks in several places in the Rim. Once proven they went private, taking on contracts with freighters. Obviously, they'd driven all kinds of cargo sections to strange places before. Despite Erik's complaining, they were fast and professional.

"Keep tracking them," Lehana instructed Kali. "Let me know when they've touched down."

"Acknowledged."

"Has the hull been reconfigured to show our new name?"

"The *Mary Bowers* is now displayed in a feminine, luxury cruiser type font," Kali confirmed.

Lehana thanked the stars for her extra payment on the hull design when she first got the *Phoenix*. Instead of painting on the name, there was a re-imager behind a translucent plate that could change the name at will. Currently she had sixteen different ship names stored, each one with its own unique type font and colors. In addition, the entire hull was now a metallic swirl of sky blue, barely pink, and deep purple.

"Adira, let Kollaiyar station know that the *Mary Bowers* is requesting permission to dock. Two occupants will need a shuttle to the planet for shopping."

"And the names of the two crew members," Adira asked. "Please don't make us silly fake celebrity types."

"What a good idea," Lehana said, chuckling. "But I won't do that. Unfortunately, I will not be making this trip down. It's not safe for me or you. If someone is looking for me they will not only have pictures but DNA comparison. I can fake my looks but I can't fake new DNA. I'll ask Stambuli to go with you."

"What if she's still working on the miner's children?"

"She'll be done by the time we land. Or..." Lehana stopped herself saying they'd be dead. She might be hardened to life and death and she had no bond with these stowaways. But she wasn't sure about Adira.

Adira was silent for a bit, her head down, as if she had finished Lehana's thought on her own.

"And what about the Q purchasing negotiations?" When Adira finally spoke, her voice was a little too bright.

"That will have to wait for a different day, a different place where I have more time to truly disguise myself and set up a new corporation. Today, we are just getting supplies and food."

Adira nodded.

"Time to Kollaiyar?" Lehana asked Kali.

"Four hours, fifty six minutes."

"Better check on our stowaways," Lehana said, standing slowly. All the adrenaline she'd used earlier in the day drained from her. "Monitor Erik and Kire for me. Ping me in the med bay when they've finally landed on Nedra and are secured in their pod."

"I will."

Lehana looked at Adira again. She had the posture of someone who had given up. "It's going to be okay," she said. "Once the twins are down and okay, you should get a nap. Be fresh for your shuttle down to Kollaiyar. Dream of real food so you have a good shopping list."

Adira smiled slightly, the kind of smile that didn't reach the eyes.

Lehana nodded and turned. She'd never been the nurturing type. She really didn't know how to do it. Alway look out or number one was her motto. Yet she'd found herself reaching out to Adira and now she had these strange feelings about protecting her. From what, she didn't know. It wasn't like Adira knew nothing of the world. She knew too much for a young woman.

She walked a little faster. Then came to a complete stop at the med bay door. And now what was she going to do? She didn't need a miner and two scrubbies on this ship. The miner might work out. He wasn't hard to look at and he seemed pretty compliant. For now.

But the children. This ship was never built to house scrubbies. Maybe if they were ten or twelve. Better yet fifteen or sixteen, she could find something for them. They could at least be useful.

What the freeze was she thinking? She rolled her head around her shoulders and shook her arms and hands until her entire body was moving and stretching. Then she slapped each side of her face, as if making sure she was awake. What was wrong with her? She'd gone soft in the last couple of days. First Adira and now this lot.

The fact was, this ship wasn't made for children. She'd never intended to have children here. She'd never hired a crew with children, and the one time she had a partnered pair she made a strict rule that no procreation was allowed. There would be no pregnancies, no births, nothing to create a scrubby. Sex was fine, but they all signed on for the shot that ensured no babies would show up.

There, decision made. She'd have to put them out. That's all there was to it. Not on Kollaiyar, of course. She wouldn't put innocents on a planet that trafficked in pirates and smugglers, prostitutes and thieves. She wasn't that uncaring. But they'd find a place. That's what she would tell the miner. He and his children would be dropped at the first safe place she could find.

She stood tall, stacked her spine one vertebrae at a time until she was as tall and strong as a conifer specimen at the Earth Conservatory. She squared her shoulders and pressed the comms. "Captain Saar, entering," she said, making sure her voice was commanding.

The door snicked open and she stepped inside.

CHAPTER 9

The door closed behind Lehana and she stayed glued to the spot just inside, suddenly unwilling to move or speak.

The man's head bent forward with both palms covering his eyes. His breathing stuttered between audible sobbing episodes. Stambuli talked to him in a low tone while rubbing one hand in circles on his back.

Lehana looked away, scanning for the two cryounits. They were both opened and empty in a corner. Slowly she moved her eyes to the area where three med slabs were kept for crew treatment. On one was a child who looked to be a toddler, or maybe a little older. He was pale, but looked to be sleeping peacefully. Lehana scanned the monitor above him. Steady rhythm. Breathing consistent. She wasn't sure if the rates listed was normal for child or not but there was no distress signals she could see.

On the other slab was a baby. It was in a medical stasis

chamber with tubes to provide oxygen and a pump to force air into lungs. Lehana couldn't tell the baby's age, but it obviously was not well. The skin had a yellow undertone with a light blue tinge to it. Had it died and Stambuli was trying to bring it back? She'd seen that blueish tone in people who were close to death. Again she scanned the monitor. The heart rate was fine for a few beats then it would have an erratic blip, then be fine again. Not a good sign.

Drakh! She couldn't tell this man he and his children would be put off at the first safe station. Not today. Maybe tomorrow.

Lehana strained to hear what Stambuli was saying.

"It's still too early to know," she said. "I've never seen cryo done on anyone younger than two. We need to be patient. I've searched the database. There is no literature on this procedure. No one has registered cryo inducement on an infant."

Lehana locked her jaw to stop herself from expressing any concern or condolences. She would not say anything yet. She didn't care about these people. She should not allow herself to care about this man or his children. It was not her problem. He'd gotten himself into this mess. It wasn't her responsibility to fix it.

She inched toward the door, careful not to make a noise as her hand reached behind her feeling for the door open switch.

Stambuli looked up. "Captain. I didn't hear you come in."

Lehana raised her chin. "It seems I've come at a bad time. I can wait to interview the prisoner later. What would you suggest? An hour? Two? We are due at Kollaiyar station in approximately four hours. When you are able to get away, I need to speak to you about a change in plans."

"What…what change in plans?" The man spoke haltingly, his head still bowed but his hands now rested on his thighs. He raised his face to look in her direction. Though his eyes were red from crying, he stared at her, demanding she pay attention. "Are you putting us off the ship at Kollaiyar station? Are you sentencing my daughter to death by removing her from this med bay?"

"I have no intention of putting anyone off except two people who will go in and do some shopping," Lehana responded in a clipped tone. How dare he accuse her of no compassion. "Stambuli is to be one of them."

The man stood, his fists clenched at his side. "She can't leave," the man said. "She is needed here. I will not allow her to leave."

"You what?" Lehana asked loudly and strode forward to within half a meter of where he stood. "You will not allow it? Who do you think is in charge here? It is certainly not the stowaway who has cost me a bonus of over one hundred million DICs. It is certainly not the man who doesn't care enough for his own children that he brings them aboard a freighter without knowing anything about the ship, the captain, or the destination. How dare you question my position or any order I make. I could order Stambuli to turn off all life support in an instance. Do you understand me?"

The man froze for a moment. She was unsure if this was the moment before he went crazy or if she had gotten through to him. She grasped the hilt of the knife she kept hidden in the back of her vest just in case.

Then he slumped back into the chair. "I apologize." His voice was quieter and not demanding. However, his posture was still on alert and he no longer looked at her. He stared at some point at the other end of the room. Not at his children but at the space where the cryounits were laid open.

He turned his face to hers and she noticed the deep blue eyes with specs of gold. She gasped and took a step back. This was the miner she'd met on Ydro-Down when she first stepped off the ship—the one that had used some kind of scanner or taser on her when he touched her elbow. The current through her suit, the flash of light in her eyes replayed quickly in her mind.

"You are correct," he continued in a slow, but deliberate manner.

This was no longer the face of defeat. It was the face of a man who was angry, a man holding tightly to his control. He suddenly seemed larger, more substantial. He was easily a head taller than Erik.

"I have no rights aboard this ship, just as I had no rights on Ydro-Down," he continued. "I am your property as I was theirs. You can choose to kill me or let me live, and the same with my children, just as the masters at Ydro-Down reminded me every day of the forty-five turns I was enslaved there."

Fort-five years as a slave was unheard of. How did he survive so long? She slowly shook her head to deny his comparison. She was no slave master. She'd never keep someone against their will unless they tried to harm her.

"Just as they reminded me when my wife was dying nearly eight turns ago." Though he spoke without raising his voice, the words were enunciated clearly with his jaw taut, his breath audible as it rushed from his nose with each new sentence.

"Just as they reminded me when I protested them putting a child not even four years old and a six-month-old baby in cryosleep only moments after my wife died. Just as they reminded me every day I went to the mines and every night I was forced to work two and sometimes three shifts. They reminded me of their power over life and death if I dared to question my food rations or made a request for medical care. Their greed for power knew no boundaries."

Then he stood and put his arms out to each side, exposing his wide chest. "Do as you wish, oh great master captain. Our lives are in your hands." Then he kneeled on the ground and prostrated himself before her. "I am ready for the whip. I ask only that you spare my children."

Drakh! He was good. Was this practiced drama or did he really believe she had no heart?

"Get up," she ordered him.

When he finally rose to stand before her again, he was no longer angry. He stood before her without apology now, forcing her to look, forcing her to see him as a man. And that was a problem. At this moment he looked more frightening than Hellebor had ever been. His willingness to sacrifice himself for his children's freedom called to her in a way she couldn't explain. She found herself jealous of the love he described between himself and his wife. She wanted to pound it out of him. She wanted to make him take it back, make him accept what she knew—the world was an evil and dark place and their was no justice or compassion.

She paced back and forth trying to put the swirling thoughts in her head into words without showing weakness. She would not play into his little game. If it was a game.

"That was a fine bit of theater you just displayed," she finally said. "But I am untouched by it. Was even one word of your story true?"

The man blinked as if he didn't understand the question. Then he swallowed and a long sigh issued from his mouth. "Every word was true," he said, his voice now sounding weary though his demeanor still was not that of defeat. "Why would a man soon to die tell anything but truth?"

"I can think of many reasons one might lie," she said. "I do it all the time."

"I bet you do," he agreed. "But whether I lie or tell the truth, you don't care. You are incapable of caring. So what does it gain me? A woman who easily flirts with a man like Scraff, a man who would kill you if you didn't comply to his demands, cannot understand truth. You deal in pretense, manipulation. A woman like that has no morals, no heart that can comprehend love or commitment."

Her heart seemed to seize for a moment. She had morals. Maybe not his morals, but she had a code—a line she wouldn't cross. And she could comprehend love more than he would ever know. That's exactly why she vowed not to love anyone or anything again when she was six years old and taken by Hellebor.

"You don't know me," she said between gritted teeth.

"I do," he said. "I know your type. I've seen men and women like you willing to do whatever it takes to get the next one million DICs. You'll cheat, steal, prostitute yourself to get that next credit. You can't afford loyalty, compassion, and certainly not commitment to anyone or any cause except yourself."

He wasn't completely wrong, she admitted to herself, except the prostitution part. She never did that. But she remained silent.

"Four thousand of us left Sol Prime on a generation ship to get away from people like you. We left Sol Prime as the Oblivion War was working its way from one solar system to the next, each warring faction caring only to have more. More possessions, more power, more of everything even if they had to sacrifice their neighbors.

"Our colony took a chance and agreed to risk our lives for two thousand years to make a home where people cared about each other more than about money and possessions and power. We lost that gamble when we crashed on a God-forsaken planetoid ruled by the same type of people we escaped. Only a few hundred of us survived. No more than seven of us were allowed at any one mine. Of the seven who were enslaved at the mine where you crashed, I was the only survivor. My wife and five others are dead. I don't know if any of the survivors at other mines are still alive."

"I'm sorry," she said. She was taken in by his story. The more she listened, the more she connected with his plight. It wasn't that different from her own. But she wouldn't tell him that. She'd told no one what her life had been like living with the most feared pirate gang in the Rim.

"A woman like you wouldn't understand what it is like to have no money, no hope for a life beyond working the mines until you die," he continued. "A woman like you would have no comprehension of the type of love you can have for another—a love that requires you to gladly give up your life in return for theirs, even though I barely know them."

He was right. She had never known that kind of love and she never would. She would never trust enough to let any person, especially not a man, get that close to her. And having children was definitely off the list. Why would anyone choose to bring children into this star-forsaken world?

"We spent every waking moment looking for a way to escape with our son. When our daughter was conceived, neither of us knew my wife was pregnant until her sixth month. Then it was too late. We were only trying to..." He stopped, and his voice choked. He wiped tears from his eyes. "Now. Our daughter may die because of QueCorp greed."

Lehana had no words. She swallowed hard and chewed her

lip, forcing the mist in her eyes to recede. She couldn't afford to care. Not now. Not ever.

As if she had no power over her own actions, she bent to him and put her hand near his shoulder, as if to touch him. Instead she pulled it away and stepped back a couple paces. "You're right. Everything you said about me is right. I can't understand. I will *never* understand."

He raised his eyes to her once more. Beautiful dark blue eyes, sparkling with tears. Eyes the colors of a space horizon when a star illuminates the edge of a world.

She stood unmoving, mesmerized by the pull of his resilience in the face of unspeakable odds. "I may be everything you said, but I am also more than that," she said slowly, trying to pull herself back from the brink of caring. "I am not Scraff or Ming Waller. But I am not good either. You are not my slave and never will be."

"And my children?" he asked.

"They are yours and yours alone," she said.

"What does that mean?" he asked.

"It means this ship was never built for children. I don't know what to do with them. I never planned for them. It means there is no one here to help you care for them, teach them, keep them from getting in the way."

"I don't need help. I can manage on my own."

"I doubt that," she said.

His brows crinkled and he turned his head to one side but said nothing.

"That said, you are free to leave this ship at any station where we stop," she continued. "Or stay on the ship if you wish."

"I am not prepared to leave yet," he said. "My daughter is still in danger. My son needs more time to recover."

"We will be landing at Kollaiyar soon. It is a planet that is known as a safe place for pirates, smugglers, greed, and every vice you can imagine. It would not be safe for you and your children to disembark there. Once we leave Kollaiyar, I will advise you of any station or planet where we plan to stop. You may make a choice to leave at any time."

He said nothing for some time.

She should leave. She'd already said too much. No need to stay here. She turned to leave.

"And if I choose to stay?" His voice drew her back and he stood. She'd never met a man who was filled with compassion and love, yet strong enough to persist in the face of hope-lessness.

His substantial size, at least half a meter taller than herself, could be used to try to subdue her. The outline of a firm musculature was detailed in his arms and legs. His torso had not a single ounce of fat. The work in the mines had kept him strong and lean.

She recognized that if he took her by surprise he could easily throw her against a wall if he wanted. Yet he didn't choose to intimidate her with his body in that way. No matter what had happened in his time on Ydro-Down, he had never become a slave on the inside. He had never accepted that as an identity.

"What will be my duties?" he asked.

Drakh. She was actually contemplating assigning him duties as a member of her crew. That had not been her plan when she walked into the med bay. Why would he stay? She never thought he would want to stay.

"Do you have any skills for space travel?" She used the same gruff tone she would to any potential crew member she'd consider hiring.

"I was top of my class as a navigator. However, that was more than two thousand years ago. As I haven't been off Ydro-Down since our ship crashed, I don't know current technologies, propulsion systems, or even the Salty Way section designations in the Rim. But I do have the ability to see the universe and spacetime without disorientation. I don't know why, but I can."

Lehana laughed wryly. "Great. I have a wormy miner asking to be a navigator. You didn't have a knockout drug to take while stuffed in that cargo compartment. Right?" She turned to Stambuli. "Have you scanned him? He would have entered the wormhole with nothing to give him a sense of reality. Is he wormy? Is his brain starting to miss connections?"

"I performed a preliminary scan," Stambuli said. "I found nothing wrong."

"I am not wormy," the man confirmed.

Stambuli pulled up his scan and pointed to a picture of his brain. "See here? There is slightly heightened activity in the reticular activating system, particularly the dorsolateral prefrontal cortex, and a slightly higher activation of the amygdala."

"And what does that mean?" Lehana asked.

"I'm not a hundred percent sure," Stambuli admitted. "Usually that heightened activity is seen in lucid dreaming. Yet clearly the man is not dreaming and is completely conscious. It may be a mistaken reading as he is under great physical and emotional stress at this moment in time and that would explain the activation of the amygdala which might also activate the DLPFC."

"I repeat, I'm not wormy and I'm not dreaming," the man said. "It is simply a skill I have. When we went through the wormhole, I saw the universe past and future and could immediately draw the safest route through."

"And was our route the safest in your estimation?"

"It was a good route, but not the best," he said with confidence.

"Right." She drew out the word. "And unfortunately there is no way to prove this because we've already passed through." She pointed at herself. "I also see the universe past and future every time we pass through the wormhole. But that doesn't mean I have a different route selection than what Kali has calculated. Have you ever piloted a ship with your suggested route?"

"No," he admitted. "As I said, I haven't been on a ship for more than two millennia. This was the first one."

"Then I think we will continue to depend on Kali's calculations."

"You can trust me to learn the navigation system quickly. I can be of service. Or I can cook, or clean, or anything else you want to assign me."

"You've already made a decision to stay?"

"For now it is the best choice for my children. I don't need charity. I just need a chance. Please, you can trust me."

"Trust." Lehana rolled the word out slowly. "I trust no one. Ever." She blew out a breath. Ever since they blew their wad in the wormhole and crashed on Ydro-Down, nothing was going her way.

"This what I'll agree to do. I will give you an opportunity to learn, and if Kali says you have enough skills to navigate I will give you a chance. After we clear Kollaiyar and are in a place where a mistake won't get us all killed."

"Kali?" he asked. "Is that the woman who was here before?"

"No, that was Adira." She spoke into the air. "Kali introduce yourself to… what is your name?"

"My real name or my number?"

"Your name, of course," she said.

"Kash Trider. My children are Eijaz and Z-Huang."

"I am Kali, the ships artificial intelligence unit." The voice came through unseen speakers in the med bay. "I have recorded your name and that of your children. I can train you in any aspect of ships duties you require, from navigation to environmental controls and medic to chef. I can access all intragalactic databases on any subject you desire. In the event the captain is unavailable, I can run the ship alone."

"The captain will never authorize you to run the ship alone," Lehana corrected. "If I was unavailable you would assist the second in command."

"I stand corrected," Kali said. "I meant to say if the ship had no crew I could run it alone based on your stored instructions."

Once again Lehana wondered if Kali needed an update. It seemed that in the AI's continued learning to build appropriate language to make humans feel comfortable, she was using more language showing self-agency.

"Thank you," Kash said, temporarily delaying Lehana's concerns with Kali's programming. "I will let you know when I am ready for instruction. Captain, how should I address you?"

"We use first names between all crew members. You may call me Lehana."

"Are you sure?" he asked. "That seems rather…informal."

"I'm not sure," she responded honestly. "However, if you are to be a member of this crew for any period of time, it is only fair that you are treated in the same way as all other crew. That includes a share in profits."

"Profits?" Kash asked.

"When we make deliveries on contract. When we buy at wholesale and sell goods for retail."

"I understand the concept of profit. I didn't understand the sharing of those profits."

Of course he wouldn't understand, Lehana realized. A slave never had anything. "The rule on my ship is that I take forty percent of all profit, and the other sixty percent is shared equally among the crew. There is no hierarchy or rank among the crew when it comes to pay. The sixty percent pay is evenly distributed. When I ask an individual to do something above and beyond the usual danger we encounter, I will pay a hazard bonus to that one person."

Kash stood before her his mouth ajar, as if he couldn't quite process what she'd said.

"Your children would not be considered crew members nor share in the profit."

"Of course," he said.

"I do have a request, in terms of address. Your children shall address me as Captain. I cannot stomach the thought that a scrubby would call me by my first name."

Kash chuckled lightly. She was surprised to hear it.

"Of course," he said. "In my culture, children are taught to respect their elders. In that regard they call adults by proper names such as Mr. Saar, Mrs. Saar, or individual Saar. In your case Captain Saar."

"Captain is sufficient."

"May I ask one more question?" Kash said.

"Yes."

"Previously you said you needed the medic."

"No, I said I needed Stambuli," she corrected.

"Yes." He turned to the medic. "I apologize, Stambuli. It will take me some time to get used to this new freedom of equals."

Stambuli smiled and bowed from her great height, almost a third taller than Kash. "I welcome you to our crew, Kash. I am not offended. Trust me when I say I will do everything possible to save your daughter. But there is nothing I can do now. We must wait at least twenty-four hours before trying to wake her again."

Kash turned back to Lehana. "You said you needed Stambuli to go to the surface. Clearly she is needed here. I volunteer to go instead so she may continue to tend to my daughter."

"I cannot allow that," Lehana said.

"May I ask why?"

She took a deep breath. She'd invited him in as a member of her crew. Only the stars knew what possessed her to do that when only moments ago she was swearing she'd dump him at the first safe station. She might as well tell him everything at this point. He had a right to know.

"You may know that the punishment for stealing a slave is death," she said.

"Yes, but you didn't steal me."

"Technically, that is true," she acknowledged. "However, I did steal Adira—even though she wished to come. And no matter the circumstances with you, I am already accused and found guilty of stealing you and your children as well. That means that both my image and my DNA are now available to any vac tracker looking for a lucrative contract. As is your image, that of your children, and all of your DNA as well. Believe me, QueCorp will make the contract very lucrative. Probably one hundred million DICs minimum."

Kash was quiet.

"Obviously, you see the dilemma. We need supplies and Stambuli is the only person they aren't seeking."

"What about that gruff person who found me, or the other person—the woman who had a gun pointed at me?"

"Kire and Erik," Lehana clarified. "They are on the dark side of a moon with the cargo we've let go, waiting our return."

"If Kollaiyar is as dangerous a place as you say, then Stambuli should not go alone," Kash said. "If only one person is to go, I volunteer. I will be careful not to touch anything, not to leave DNA to be traced. If I am captured I will not reveal you or the ship. If I don't return, you can leave and promise to find a good home for my children."

Stambuli put a hand lightly on Kash's shoulder. "I am capable of facing many attackers at the same time. I have extensive training. I may appear compliant, but I can assure you I will fight to the death if necessary."

Lehana looked from Kash to Stambuli. Damn him! What was he doing to her? Making her question her own decisions? But he was right.

"He's right," Lehana said aloud. "It's my problem. I should be the one taking the risk. Not you. You are needed here. I know Kollaiyar as if it were my home. I spent plenty of time here growing up, learning my trade. I would know where to go to hide, who to contact I found myself in trouble."

"Are you sure?" Stambuli asked. "I am not afraid."

"You should be afraid," Lehana said. "No one on Kollaiyar can be trusted. No one."

"I will go with you," Kash said. "You are as important to my children as Stambuli. If you were lost, who would run the ship? Who else on the crew has the experience to do the jumps, to negotiate trades, to keep us ahead of any trackers?"

Lehana faced him and put her hands on his shoulders has Stambuli did. She grasped him tighter and shook lightly. "Listen to me. I promise that..."

She let go and stepped away quickly, shaken. Then slouched to the floor as if her legs would no longer hold her. When she'd grabbed him, an electrical current moved from his shoulders to her fingers and up her arm directly into her mind. It was the same feeling of disorientation she'd felt when she first met him, only much worse.

He bent to her and took her hand. "You felt it too," he said quietly. "You saw spacetime when we touched."

She wrenched her hand away. "What are you doing to me? What power is this? What are you?"

"It used to happen with my wife as well," he said softly. "I thought it was because we loved each other so deeply. Clearly that is not the case here."

"Clearly," she said. "Stambuli, scan me. Tell me if anything is changed."

Stambuli pulled her to a standing position and helped her to the third slab. "Please recline."

Lehana lay flat on her back.

"Be still." She ran the scanner over her body. "Everything is functioning normally. However, your brain is showing heightened levels of oxytocin, prolactin and endorphins. Any chance you just had an orgasm?"

Lehana shot straight up. "Of course not. I barely touched him. How could I?"

"Obviously not because of sex, but these are the same levels one would expect after an orgasm."

"It. Was. Not. An orgasm," Lehana emphasized. "Believe me, I know what that feels like. It doesn't feel like this."

"It is not something my wife and I experienced in our relationship either before we were put in cryosleep for our trip to the Rim. However, once we were on Ydro-Down we experienced this regularly, just by prolonged touching. It is even more intense during sexual intercourse."

"It was not an orgasm," Lehana repeated. She covered her eyes with the back of her hand. How did she get into these dilemmas? By the stars she never asked for this.

"I have a supposition," Kali said.

"Please, suppose away," Lehana said. "It can't be any worse than this reality."

"There are reports of certain cryoborn with this ability. Those who have been tested had one commonality. That is they were all in cryosleep when the quantum wave from the Q-bombs passed through the Salty Way. Adults, upon awakening, noticed this phenomena when touching another cryoborn. Though it is intense between two cryoborn partners, it is even more so between a cryoborn and a non-cryoborn partner. There are only three substantiated cases of a cryoborn and non-cryoborn's reactions during sexual intercourse. Shall I describe the sensations reported in that case?"

"No!" Both Kash and Lehana said at the same time.

Her entire body flushed with desire at the thought of having Kash beneath her. If what she felt in that brief moment of his touch was any indication, she wouldn't survive sex with him.

"No problem then," Lehana said, a little louder than she'd planned. "All I have to do is avoid touching him ever again."

"These same three cryoborn and non-cryborn studies also report that touching during navigation of a wormhle increases the percentage of perfect traverses to nearly one hundred percent, and in shorter timeframes, and without the side effects of disorientation."

"Are you sure those are true reports?" Lehana asked. "What I just felt was worse than traversing a wormhole without drugs."

"But we weren't in a wormhole when we touched," Kash said. "If we were, perhaps it would be different. Better."

Lehana stared straight at him. "That is not going to happen. I've done perfectly fine on my own with Kali's calculations. There is no need to ever repeat this little experiment. No touching, and that's final."

Kash stood less than a meter from her and his head was slightly cocked to one side with a half grin.

"That won't be a problem for you, correct, Kash?"

"Touching you will never be a problem, Lehana."

CHAPTER 10

Kash and Lehana carefully kept the shopping bot in front of them as they made their way into the food market and selected purchases for the next three weeks.

"Something wrong?" Kash asked. "You are obviously uneasy and keep looking behind us."

"Other than kicking myself for agreeing to let you come, you mean?"

"I didn't force you. You knew this was the only safe possibility."

She stepped past him and turned so she could look behind them again. She pointed to an onion toward the top of the table. "There are two people who have seemed to follow us since we entered the marketplace twenty minutes ago. They are always two to three stalls behind; but every turn we've made they have made."

"I'm going to check on those oranges." Kash moved past Lehana to another table.

She turned to watch him walk away. Damn, ever since that

suggestion of sex with Kash had entered her mind she couldn't shake it. She'd never had mind-blowing sex. She'd never been able to let go of her fears of trust and commitment. With Kash maybe she could experience it without trust and commitment.

Drakh. That was a slippery thought to follow. She needed to concentrate. Lehana looked in the direction of the orange stand, Kash picked up an orange to inspect. He leaned toward the person behind the table to ask a question. Then he motioned for her to join him. She took a deep breath and vowed to think only of oranges.

"The vendor says these are real," he said. "But I want a taste to be sure. She's demanding payment up front."

Lehana looked at the vendor and held up her DIC key waiting for the vendor to change her mind.

The vendor's eyes widened, as expected, when she noticed the symbol at the bottom of the key Lehana held. A tiny red symbol was an indicator that she had more than a hundred million credits at her disposal.

The woman quickly cut the orange into slices and displayed them on a plate. "Taste please," she said. "We have as many real oranges as you need."

Kash held a slice up to her mouth. She carefully bit into the glistening flesh of the orange, being sure not to let her lips touch his fingers, leaving the rind in his hand. Her eyes widened as the juice squirted into her throat.

"Real?" he asked.

She nodded, unable to speak as she enjoyed the taste of orange and the closeness of Kash. The idea of sharing the taste with him through her lips took over and she leaned toward him.

He lowered his head. But instead of kissing her, he whispered in her ear. "No touching, remember? I see the people following us. We need to make a large purchase here and then pretend to walk toward the ship, while doubling back on them."

She stiffened and berated herself for her lack of control in that moment. When they got back to the ship, she'd ask Stambuli what she could take to stop this craving for him.

"We'll take fourteen kilos of these oranges," Lehana said, abruptly turning to the vendor. She held out her key to pay.

"Do you have a shopping bot for pickup?" the vendor asked.

"Yes, number ninety-two. You'll see the crest of the *Mary Bowers* on it."

As she and Kash turned to walk away from their followers, Lehana tapped her comms and connected with Adira aboard the ship. "We have two new friends we need to greet," she said. "We're going to buy one more item and then the bot should be on its way within a couple minutes. Unload it quickly and get Kali primed for leaving the minute we hit the doors. We may have uninviteds trying to crash the party."

"Got it. I think," Adira responded. "

"How do you like sausage?" Kash asked when Lehana disconnected.

"Depends. Real or synth?"

Kash chuckled. "I prefer real," he said and pointed to the sausage stand near the entrance to an alley. "I'm thinking the crew could come up with a number of good dishes."

As they walked toward the sausage stand, Lehana uncoiled her hair and let it flow across her shoulders. "It's show time. Follow my lead."

They quickly purchased a mixture of twenty percent real pork and eighty percent synthed pork. The bot was already there waiting. Once loaded on the bot, they paid the extra DICs for air transfer of all the purchases to the *Mary Bowers*. If they had to run, neither wanted to leave all that good food behind.

"Friends? Thieves? Or trackers?" Lehana asked as she sashayed toward their two followers.

"I'm betting trackers," Kash said.

"I completely agree. The question is if they are tracking us."

"Perhaps we should ask."

"Yes, but not until we have them in a place where my proposition won't be observed by too many others."

"Definitely don't want to share you with anyone else," Kash said easily.

Soon they had stepped into the alley, and the two individuals were at the last merchant table possible.

"Now, it's magic time," Lehana said. "Stay back here and look scared."

"I think I should be the one to approach them, you stay here."

Lehana looked up to his strong face. "What are you carrying?"

"Carrying?" Kash asked.

"Weapons? I know I didn't give you a gun. Knife? Tranquilizer?"

"Fists, kicks, choke holds," he responded.

"That would make a scene, wouldn't it? Something we can't afford. I've done this before. I know how men think. Stay here."

"You don't know how this man thinks," he mumbled as she walked toward the two men, her hips swaying suggestively. Kash inched a little closer so he could hear clearly, not sure he wanted to know all her tricks.

"Excuse me," Lehana said in a low voice, with a slight tremble. "We just lost communication with our ship and I'm unsure if we're heading in the right direction to get back to the shuttle for space dock."

The two men looked at each other nervously without speaking. Then one shrugged his shoulder and swallowed.

"You're...uh...going the wrong way," the shoulder-shrugger said.

"Really?" Lehana asked, her voice pitched to be sultry as if inviting a proposition. "I could have sworn we had to go down this alley."

The other man smiled with confidence, and moved forward, closing the space between him and Lehana. He lifted her chin carefully. "We could help you get there, for a small price."

Lehana pretended to be shaken by his touch as she silently removed a blaster from his waistband and turned it on him, pushing it firmly into his chest. "What price would that be?"

Kash quickly moved in to stand beside the other man. He pressed a small needle into his neck and supported him as he slouched against him. He threw the one of the man's arms over his shoulder and began walking him further into the alley like he was supporting a drunk.

Lehana pushed the blaster in the first man's chest again. "Let's follow your friend. He seems to have a problem standing up."

Finding a darkened space between two buildings, Kash placed the dead weight of the man upright, propped against a wall.

"Sit down," Lehana said to her charge. "We have some questions." She flicked a glance at Kash. "What did you give him?"

"Something Stambuli gave me. She likes my need for truth."

"Is there more?" she asked.

Kash retrieved a vial from his pocket. "She said it was enough for up to four doses."

"What a good medic she is," Lehana said. "I think I'll keep her around."

"I think there's a misunderstanding," the first man said as his unconscious partner fell head first into his lap. "Whoever you think we are, you're wrong."

"Is that so?" Lehana asked. "So you weren't planning to force me into sex a few minutes ago?"

"Sex?" Kash said loudly. "Why would you want sex with him when you have me? One touch and it's everything you ever wanted."

"I…I didn't know what you wanted," the man said.

"If you didn't want sex, why were you following her around for the past hour?" Kash asked.

"We weren't following anyone," the man sputtered. "We were shopping. I didn't even notice her until she asked us for directions."

"Is that true?" Kash asked as he aspirated another needle. "I'm a stickler for the truth."

"Oh, he is," Lehana said. "And he wants the whole truth, no half truths and half lies."

The man groaned. "Is that what I think it is?"

Kash nodded.

"You don't have to use it on me. I'll tell you the truth."

"I know you will," Kash said as he plunged it into the man's neck.

With both now unconscious, Lehana and Kash pulled them further down the alley.

Lehana pointed to a pleasure house two doors down. "Do you know what that is?"

Kash shook his head. "This planet isn't the kind of place I visited with my wife."

"It's a pleasure house," Lehana said. "As in pay for whatever you want."

"Oh. I'm…uh…not interested. Don't you think we just need

to wait until they wake up and then ask the questions and get on our way? I'm...I guess...old-fashioned when it comes to pleasuring a woman."

Lehana chuckled in a low tone, trying not to be conspicuous. "You really are a good man, aren't you."

"I like to think so."

"No, I mean really good. Like never cheated on your wife. Never lusted after a younger woman."

"Why would I cheat on the woman I love?" he asked. "When I commit to someone, that one individual is more than enough for me."

"And the lust?" she pressed.

"I admit to thinking about the occasional other individual, but never more than a passing thought. And never once considered exploring it further."

"Like I said, a good man." She sighed loudly. "A too good man."

"What does that mean?"

"Nothing. Now listen, we are going to need privacy to question these two."

"Just ask questions?" Kash confirmed. "Nothing more. No expectations of..."

"Of course," Lehana said. "I meant it when I said there would be no touching between us."

Kash slung the larger man over his shoulder, and helped Lehana drag the other one up to the door.

Lehana held up her DIC key.

The door went transparent but did not open. A naked woman bot appeared on the other side. "We don't do dead bodies. No matter the price."

"No, no. These are for us," Lehana said. "And they aren't dead. Just...compliant."

"This is a bot sex house. Not human on human sex."

"You have pleasure rooms, don't you?" Lehana asked.

"Yes. Rooms for bots and humans."

"We will pay for a room without bots."

"Strange. Want room but no bot sex."

"We're…different," Lehana added. "We just want one room for the four of us."

"Will charge kink fee of five hundred per individual and double standard room price for a foursome."

"Any discount for not using a bot?" Lehana asked, always looking for a better deal. "Saves on maintenance."

"Discounts are not part of our programming. No discounts ever. Gold service always." The door now presented the keycode. "Total four thousand five hundred credits."

Lehana held her DIC key to the door to transfer the credits. The door then turned green and let them enter.

A second naked bot, this one built like a man, appeared next to the one that greeted them. He had a double gurney for two. "I will deliver your sex partners to room twenty-eight. Please follow."

The two bots easily lifted the two unconscious men onto the gurney. Lehana and Kash walked behind. Once they reached the stark white room the bot unloaded the two men onto a large bed with two spotlights from the ceiling bathing them in white light.

"Are there particular colors you prefer in your pleasure room?" the bot asked.

Kash looked at Lehana, his eyes wide. "Colors?"

"Red," Lehana said. "Definitely red."

"Really?" Kash asked. "Why not something soothing, calming…like blue or green?"

"One of each, perhaps?" the bot said and one of the spotlights now cast a red light and the other blue. "Will you be using one partner or switching? I can set the controls to switch if you are going to trade and wish to keep the color of your choice."

Kash boggled. "Are you serious? This is a joke, right?"

"I apologize," the bot said. "I did not mean to make a joke. My programming does not include jokes."

Lehana couldn't help laughing aloud.

Kash stared at her until she calmed herself.

"This is my friend's first time," Lehana said. "I'm…um…his trainer. That is why we are using compliant humans. So he can learn to give full pleasure."

"A virgin. I understand," the bot said.

"I am not a virgin," Kash said, his voice a bit peeved.

"Not exactly a virgin. Just not experienced in different… uh…pleasuring practices."

"I understand," the bot said again and then he opened a cabinet and pointed to the area of colorful objects ranging from feathers to handcuffs and dildos to a large variety of vibrators and pulsators. "You may wish to try each of these to learn what is pleasurable before attempting to demonstrate with the other humans."

Kash shook his head. "I don't need any of those things."

"And, should the two humans be unable to perform," the bot continued and pointed to the array of pulsators and the finger vibrators, "these will help to ensure the two of you have a very pleasurable experience. Of course, for only three thousand DICs more you could also ask me to return. I am much better than a human and can ensure multiple orgasms."

"Multiple?" Lehana asked and smiled at Kash.

"As many as you can handle," the bot confirmed. "Shall I demonstrate?"

Lehana chuckled again and looked at Kash, reveling in his

obvious discomfort. "Though it sounds *very* appealing, I'll have to decline. I was hired explicitly to train him with humans. If the men can't perform for demonstration purposes, I'll have to take him in my own hands.

The bot bowed. "Of course. I will leave you."

"One more thing," Lehana said.

"Yes?"

"What is the charge to haul the men out of the room when our time is up?"

"It is not in our service package to deliver unconscious men to the street," the bot said. "If they should perish before becoming conscious we are held liable. We are allowed to bring in an unconscious but living person if you guarantee they will be alive and well before you leave."

"They'll both be conscious," Lehana assured the bot. "Conscious and compliant."

"We will need to confirm they are alive and able to walk before you leave," the bot said. "If any human dies while you are in the pleasure room, we lock down the room and report it to the Kollaiyar authorities You are each charged a one million credit fee and held until the authorities arrive. Do you understand?"

Both Kash and Lehana nodded.

After a moment, the bot held the keycard out to her. "Assuming they are conscious and able to walk on their own, we will escort them to the exit and arrange for a transport if needed. The charge will be five hundred DICs each. However, if they are still unconscious we will charge the death fee and contact authorities."

"Agreed." Lehana held up her key once again to transfer another one thousand DICs to the pleasure house account.

"Thank you for your business." The bot feigned an awkward

smile and finally exited the room.

"Help strip them them," Lehana instructed as soon as the bot was out of the room.

"I thought he'd never shut up with his rules and fees. Are all pleasure houses run like this?" Kash roughly stripped the man who had begun to proposition Lehana.

"Unfortunately, no." Lehana quickly stripped the other man and arranged him to half sitting on pillows. "Kollaiyar, despite being a pirate haven, takes good care of their pleasure workers—bots or humans. The pleasure business is their one fully lawful enterprise and they don't want anyone looking beyond it. Everything else sold on this planet is likely purloined rather than purchased on the legitimate market."

She walked over to the closet of toys and pulled out two sets of fur-lined handcuffs. She tossed them to Kash and he fumbled the catch.

"You said we were not…"

"Cuff them together," she said. "One arm each and one foot each. They'll look better with a little fur."

"Right, the two of them." He quickly did what she asked.

She pulled a chair to the end of the bed, kicked back and put her feet up. "Now we wait for them to wake up."

Kash pulled up a chair next to her. Instead of putting his feet on the bed he angled toward her and stared.

Lehana cleared her throat. "Not exactly how you pictured this shopping outing?"

"No."

"Truth. You've never been to a pleasure house? Not even to walk in and see what it's all about?"

"Never saw the need."

"Yep. Too good a man."

"What do you mean by that?" he asked. "You say it like it's a bad thing.

"Just hard to believe. I've heard of men like you, from Hellebor. He made it sound like it was boring and…um…not something I should ever seek."

"Hellebor? The notorious pirate?"

Damn. She'd slipped on that one.

"How do you know about him? Even Scraff was scared of him."

Drakh. She might as well come clean. Then he'd know exactly why they'd never have even an occasional sex-only, no commitment kind of relationship. Not that she could stand it with that whole electric current, disorienting thing he had going on.

"Lehana?" he asked, his voice filled with compassion.

"He's kind of like my father, in a sick kind of way."

Kash didn't say anything for a long time. Though his mouth wasn't opened in astonishment, she could practically see the wheels turning in his head as he tried to parse what she said.

"Short version of long, sordid story. Parents were killed during a raid. Hellebor was pissed about something. I'm still not sure what. I was five, or maybe just turned six. Anyway, my loving aunt and uncle made a deal with him. He could have me for a fifty-year indentureship in exchange for their lives and their children's lives. Hellebor agreed. End of story."

"Fifty?" Kash asked quietly. "At five years old?"

"No big deal," she said. "I don't blame them. I'd do the same thing if it were my kids on the line. I bet you would too."

"No. I wouldn't."

"Liar," she said, a little too loudly. "You love them. You said you would do anything for them."

"I would risk myself for them," he said. "I would indenture

myself for them. But I would never force someone else, against their will, to risk their life for them."

"You're saying that only because you haven't been faced with that decision," Lehana stated. "If I told you I could only have two children living on my ship, and Adira had one, and you had to make the choice. You would throw her kid overboard in an instant."

"I would not."

"You would," she said again. "You'd have to. That's the way the world works." When he reached for her, she shrank from his touch. "No touching, remember?" Her voice shook, not from fear but from the desire to touch him anyway. No one was so good as to sacrifice their own children for someone else's child. No one.

"I'm really sorry you grew up that way," Kash said, no longer looking at her. "There is always more than one choice. The choice your aunt made is, perhaps, understandable. But there was another choice."

"What other choice?" she asked, almost in a whisper.

"The choice to claim you as her own. The choice to look for another way. The choice to try to negotiate instead of making an offer that would hurt a five-year-old child for the rest of her life. It's a choice made from fear, not from strength."

Lehana had no response. She'd eventually accepted her aunt's decision. It was the first and last time she agreed to sacrifice herself for someone else. Kash just didn't understand. He could never understand.

One of the men groaned. "Where am I? I feel like I've been dumped from a speeding land shuttle."

"What the freeze?" the other man exclaimed, holding up their handcuffed hands.

"Drakh! We're butt naked."

"Brilliant observation," Lehana said. "Believe me when I tell you it is not a pretty sight, but I do like my subjects uncomfortable." Then she tapped her ear twice. "Kali, record interview."

A responding ping immediately echoed in her ear.

"What does that mean?" the man nearest Kash asked.

"It means you will be forced to tell us the truth," Lehana said. "Let's start with an easy one. Your name please."

"Fishel," he responded.

"Shut up," the other one said. "No names."

"What is a good name for someone who is foolish?" Lehana asked Kash.

"Wreck? Infant? Dunce?"

"Infant seems appropriate. Is that your name?" Lehana asked the man. "Infant."

"Yes, that's it," he said with great effort.

"Is Infant your real name?" Lehana asked again.

He writhed beneath her gaze. "No, it's…it's…Zelo," he blurted out under duress.

"Now that wasn't so hard, was it, Little Zelo?" Then she turned back to the more compliant man. "Why were you following us, Fishel?"

"He told me to. I do what he says."

"What else did he tell you?"

"He said if we didn't follow you and report, we'd be dead."

"Shut. Up!" Zelo said. "They can't force you to talk. They can only force you to tell the truth if you talk or even acknowledge the question with a nod or head shake."

"Oh." Fishel pushed both lips together, tucking them under.

"Who would kill you if you didn't follow through?" Lehana asked.

Fishel shook his head and kept his mouth tightly closed.

"Your boss?"

"We don't have a boss," Fishel blurted out.

"What about Zelo here?" she pressed. "Is he your boss?"

Fishel shook his head.

"He sure sounds like your boss," Kash said. "It sounds to me like he's giving you orders."

"He's not my boss. He's indentured just like me."

"Shut. Up!" Zelo said again, his jaw stiff and his free hand fisted.

"I hate to do this, but I think we need shut Zelo up. He's not being helpful." Lehana looked at Kash. "Load another syringe."

Zelo lifted his chin as if to offer his neck. "Better to be killed by drugs than by Hellebor."

"Hellebor?" Lehana said. "Now that's helpful. He's not a very nice man, is he?"

Zelo let out a string of curses for his mistake.

Fishel's eyes widened and he nodded vigorously. "We were checking DNA for four slaves. We were tracing everything you touched. One of you is the miner from Ydro-Down, right?" He looked directly at Kash. "You're the one with two kid slaves, right?"

"The orange," Lehana said.

"Sorry," Kash said. "My fault. Won't happen again."

Too bad. Because it had been good while it lasted. Lehana looked directly at Fishel. "Hellebor's tracking someone who took slaves?"

Fishel nodded.

"Is there a bonus if I turn him in?" She nodded toward Kash. "I didn't know he was a slave. I thought he'd just be good for a little tumble."

"He is pretty good looking...for a slave." Fishel said. "I can see that."

"As yummy as he is, I'd rather have the bonus. Who's

charged with stealing him? Perhaps I could find that man too and return them both for an even bigger bonus."

"The thief isn't a man, it's a woman," Fishel said.

"Shut up!" Zelo repeated.

"If she finds out on her own and turns him in, we won't get the bonus," Fishel whined. Then he turned to Lehana. "I'll tell you who it is, if you agree to handcuff the big guy and give him to me. We can share the bonus. Seventy for me and thirty for you when you turn him over to us. Agreed?"

"I want sixty," Lehana said. "I have the goods. You have nothing without me. It seems only fair I get sixty percent."

"Forty for you, sixty for me," Fishel countered. "I know the owner and I deliver. I'll give you the name of the woman and if you ever find her you let me know. You'll give her to me then I'll pay seventy to you on that one because you'll have to do the detective work."

"That sounds fair," Lehana said.

"Shut up," Zelo said, with less force this time as if he'd already given up the fight.

"The woman we're supposed to find used to be indentured to Hellebor, just like Zelo and me," Fishel said. "He told us she was so hardened that she would kill her own mother without blinking an eye. She's loyal to no one. If she had kids, they would run away from her. No man would ever touch her, because she'd been known to cut off their snake after sex."

"That sounds pretty scary," Lehana agreed, trying to stop herself from laughing. "I definitely want to know her name because I want to stay out of her way."

"Exactly. That's why you want us to turn this guy here into Hellebor for you. You don't want to get between us and Hellebor."

"So, I don't have to see Hellebor then?"

"No. You don't want to see him. He's awful," Fishel said.

"Good. I'd rather you handle everything with Hellebor." She turned to Kash. "I'm sorry to do this to you. You do understand, right? I don't want to die. I don't want to be on Hellebor's list."

Kash lowered his head and nodded. "At least I had a small taste of freedom," he said. "And I enjoyed the taste of you, too, while it lasted."

Lehana almost spit. She'd walked herself into that one.

She cleared her throat and turned back to Fishel. "What is this person's name that Hellebor seeks so I make sure never to run into her?"

"Lehana Saar," Fishel said with reverence in his voice. "She even stole one of Hellebor's ships when her indentureship was up. That's how she repayed him."

Lehana feigned a gasp. "I've never heard of her," she said with awe. "Do you know the name of her ship? I take jobs on all kinds of ships. I want to be sure to avoid hers."

"The *Phoenix*," Fishel said. "At least that is what it was called when she left Ydro-Down. She always has a freighter. That's how she makes her money. Stealing and trading."

"You got everything," Zelo finally said. "Now handcuff the guy and cut us loose. We'll forget we ever met you. Hellebor will be happy with this little bonus and once we have him we can go after his kids.

"Is Hellebor here, on Kollaiyar?" Lehana asked. "I definitely don't want to see him."

"We called him when we found the DNA," Fishel said. "He's on his way. He may even be on Kollaiyar by now. How long have we been out?"

Lehana stood. "Time to leave. I don't want meet him."

"Cut us loose now," Fishel said. "And I'll transfer your forty percent of the bonus."

"Oh, that." She looked at Kash. "I'm afraid I can't do that. You see, I kind of like this guy's action. I'm not ready to give him yet."

"What the freeze!" Fishel said. "You agreed to the deal. You said—"

"I've changed my mind." She pressed the system comms at the door. "We are ready to depart. Please confirm the two men are alive."

The door opened and the same naked male robot entered.

Lehana waved her hand in the direction of the two men. "See, alive and well. Completely conscious."

"Let us out. Let us out," the two men screamed at the same time. "They tried to kill us. Look, we are in handcuffs."

"You still have twenty three minutes left in paid time for the room rental," the bot said. "Do you wish to abandon your time?"

Lehana rolled her eyes and pointed at the two men. "Look at them. Do either of them look ready to perform? In spite of everything I did to entice them they just couldn't do anything."

The bot rolled over to the bed. "Yes. I see how they would be disappointing."

"What would be the cost for you to remain here for the next twenty minutes and just stare at them to see if anything comes up?" Lehana asked.

"Just stare?" the bot asked. "In my experience, staring doesn't usually work."

"I'm paying you just to stare at their penis. You could sing to them too. Maybe an erotic song with instructions on what they should have done."

"I do have four hundred possible songs," the bot said.

"Good. What is the price?" Lehana asked

"It is only one fifth of the time, so one fifth of my normal fee of three thousand DICs. Six hundred DICs."

"That's a steal," Lehana said with a big smile. She held up her key and transferred the funds.

"Not a minute before our paid time is up," Kash emphasized.

"Understood," the bot said. "We want you to get the full benefit of your payment."

As Kash and Lehana exited the room, she heard the bot begin singing a ditty about foreplay.

A female bot met them in the hall. "Thank you for your business. May I order you a shuttle to somewhere else on the planet? There are many fine entertainments."

"A shuttle to our ship would be nice," Lehana said.

"Done," the bot said.

Lehana held up her key again.

"No charge," the bot said. "The shuttle is included in the gold package you ordered. It will meet you at the other end of the market in three minutes. I believe you can walk quickly and make it."

"Excellent," Lehana said. "Thank you. This has been a pleasurable experience."

When they exited, Kash turned back to look at the door once more. Again it turned from transparent to opaque.

"Learn something new every day," Lehana said as she picked up the pace.

He matched her with ease. "I'm sorry about the orange. I should have been paying more attention. I was distracted by the smell. When I tasted it all I could think about was seeing your reaction…your pleasure in tasting the orange.

"It *was* a great orange. Don't beat yourself up. It worked out. If they hadn't caught your DNA they wouldn't have followed us and I wouldn't know Hellebor had the contract. Now I know who we are dealing with. Information is power."

"But Hellebor. I can't imagine how that must feel for you."

"I feel nothing," she said quickly. "Hellebor was my past. That's all. He wasn't all evil. He taught me how to stay alive. How to take care of myself. I'm grateful for that. As for the rest, let's just say I have no intention of going back to it."

"Got it," Kash said. "The subject is closed."

Lehana looked at him closely as he stared straight ahead. He really was a good man. She sighed. And she was the worst thing that could happen to him.

CHAPTER 11

*L*ehana reached the docking door first, with Kash right on her heels. She thumbed the comms at her ear. "Plot the course to Nedra and let the twins know it's going to be a fast fly-in with the cargo. I want them already off planet and in orbit when we get there."

"Already done," Kali responded. "They are lifting off now."

"I'm checking on Eijaz and Z-Huang, if you don't need me right now," Kash said.

Lehana nodded. "Thanks for everything today. You were good. Real good."

He smiled, but she noticed it didn't reach his eyes. As he walked away she knew whatever she may have temporarily fantasized about a relationship, was just that fantasy. The best thing she could do for him now was get him and his kids to safety before Hellebor found them.

"Secure the docking bay door." She watched as it hinged inward and the security light went green, then she strode to the bridge.

"Adira, get onto the bridge comms," Lehana said. "Get immediate permission for the *Mary Bowers* to leave space dock. Tell them we want tethers off now and are within a couple shakes of going to impulse power."

Adira nodded and patched into the stations transportation office.

Lehana put a hand lightly on her arm. "Don't let them give you any bureacratic drakh trying to delay you. We're doing a fly-in pick up the twins. It's going to be rough, so be sure you're strapped in well."

"Tethers are released," Kali announced, "Impulse power to engines initiated, we are pulling out of space dock."

Lehana finally took in a deep breath. She didn't dare voice the hope they'd evaded Hellebor yet. She'd celebrate once she had her extensive qubition cargo back aboard and the twins safely inside. If they could somehow manage all that in the next two to three hours they'd have a chance of losing any tail.

She pinged Stambuli. "Eijaz and Z-Huang?" she asked.

"They are stable," Stambuli answered. "Kash is here now. Neither has awakened."

"Make sure you, Kash and the kids are secure. It may be a bumpy ride back to Nedra."

"May the stars guide us safely to recover our crew and miss Hellebor's arrival," she said.

"He'll find us…eventually," Lehana said. "I just want to put off that date by a few days if I can. Give us time to think and plan."

"Initiating cargo docking sequence," Kali said.

"About time you got here," Erik said into the bridge comms. "We've seen enough of this moon to last us a lifetime."

"Welcome home," Lehana said, ignoring Erik's sarcasm. "You have twenty minutes before we move off of Nedra and try to make it to the dead zone before we pick up a tail. We are expecting a tail within the hour and don't want anything left for them to find."

"Opening cargo bay doors," Kali continued.

Lehana watched her monitor as Erik and Kire did the dance of simultaneous movement to lock in the cargo, bring the shuttle into the ship, and activate the air lock. She waited a few more minutes until the twins made it to their quarters safely.

"Maximum speed to the dead zone," she said. "Time to initial dead zone interception?"

"Thirty hours, twenty eight minutes, twelve seconds," Kali responded.

"Too long. Plot a snaked course through asteroid fields where we can play hide and seek as we make our way to the dead zone."

"That will add a minimum of ten percent to time to dead zone," Kali responded.

"Well, we can't take a straight shot. Too easy to follow our trajectory. Do the best you can."

"Asteroid field in ten minutes," Kali said. "Added time ten point one three, six, eight, nine—"

"No need to give exact to thirty decimals," Lehana reminded her. "Two or three are plenty."

Kash stepped onto the bridge and took the navigation seat next to Lehana.

She swallowed her reaction to him. When she had time she'd have the ship reconfigured to have the navigation station further away.

"Your children?" she asked.

"Stambuli believes they have passed the danger zone. She expects them to wake in eighteen to twenty-four hours if they continue to progress at the same rate."

"Good," Lehana said in a clipped tone, keeping her eyes straight ahead.

"Adira mentioned you have a cat that the children may be allowed to play with. Is that true?"

Lehana had completely forgotten about the cat. What was it's name. LaLa? No, Layla. Damn, she'd only taken it to get back at Scraff. She'd never thought what else to do with it. Adira was the primary caregiver.

She sighed. If she couldn't take care of a cat, it was proof she was not the nurturing sort and definitely not cut out for children onboard this ship. When she was a child with Hellebor, there was always a nannybot that took care of all their physical and educational needs. There were a few family units formed among members of Hellebor's gang, but she never felt a need to be part of those groups.

After her parents were killed, as far as she was concerned there was no need for parents. Some kids her age thought of Hellebor as their father, but not Lehana. What little memory she had of the five years with her parents was filled with unconditional love. Since their death she'd never had that feeling again. In fact, she questioned whether it really existed at all or is it only a part of a child's imagination.

"The cat?" Kash asked again.

"Fine. Fine," Lehana managed to get out, shaking herself from her memories. "Adira is in charge of the cat, whatever she says is fine with me. Just keep the children off the bridge and out of my way."

"Of course."

This felt like the longest ten minutes of her life—feeling pulled toward Kash, but knowing it was not natural, was a stressor she didn't need right now. Where was the damn asteroid field?

"Time to asteroid field?" Lehana asked to get her head out of noticing Kash.

"Seven minutes, twenty-two seconds." Kash reached over and tapped the screen directly in front of her with the time clearly counting down to their destination.

"Drakh!" Lehana grabbed the screen with both hands as if she was going to tear it off the desk. "I know that. How did I not see it? "

"You are feeling uncomfortable in my presence," Kash said. "Do you wish for me not to be on the bridge?"

"I am *not* uncomfortable." She forced herself to release the screen and sit back in the chair. "There's just a lot happening right now. A lot of change. A lot of stress."

"That is true. And my being here is adding to that stress."

"You are not adding to my stress," she said a little too loud with her words barely emerging between her locked teeth. What was wrong with the man? Was he purposely goading her into a fight?

Kash stood and backed away from the chair. "Is this better?"

She turned, stood, and looked straight at him and yelled, "No it's not better."

His lip quirked up, and she realized that was not what she intended to say.

"What are you trying to prove?"

He put his hands out to the side. "I'm an open book. You know my story, my secrets, my need to save my children. But you are closed tight, not even able to admit your own feelings to yourself. That is dangerous in a captain. That means you may not be making good decisions. You may not be focused because you are distracted."

"Distracted?" she asked. "By what?"

"By me." He moved to within a foot of her again. "You are distracted by the possibility I may touch you again and what you will feel."

"You will not touch me again," she emphasized. "I know that, so why would it distract me?"

"You are distracted by the fact that when I am within your sight, you now crave being near me. All you can think of is how close can I get?"

"You must really think you're something special. Do you honestly think that you are attractive to me? That you are even close to the kind of man I would consider—for even one second —having sex with?"

"I can't speak to the attraction part," Kash admitted. "But I know that you are unconsciously bending toward me, wanting me closer, and counteracting that requires every bit of concentration you possess."

"You can't know that because it's not true," she said, raising her chin.

"I know it because I feel exactly the same," he said.

Lehana shook her head vigorously, denying his words though she knew they were absolutely true. Hellebor used to tell her the best way to take control of hormones was to have wild sex for a couple days with someone. Sometimes it worked or her. Not always. She'd learned the hard way that she had to choose partners carefully. It had to be someone she was at least a little bit attracted to. Someone who would let her be in control at all times. One or two sessions and then goodbye. No repeats.

She took a long look at Kash. She was definitely attracted to him on a purely physical level. Since the incident at the pleasure palace, she thought of him far too frequently. But she was worried about the whole good man vibe. Was it possible for him to accept it's all just sex with no other expectations?

"Asteroid field in two minutes, thirty eight seconds," Kali announced.

Thank the stars! She turned away rom Kash, sat back in the chair and stared at the viewscreen in front of her. If it weren't for the timing of the asteroid field, she would do it right now just to get it over with. But she couldn't risk being disoriented right now.

Kash sat next to her at the navigation station. She felt the pull, but it wasn't as bad as before. Maybe he was right. Acknowledging its existence, even if she didn't act on it, was the first step toward concentration.

"Approaching asteroid navigation," Lehana said on the comms to all crew. "Strap in tight."

"Here we go," Kash said.

The ship lurched to one side, then another as it flew between asteroids.

"I can smooth out the ride," Kash said, "if Kali will let me take the helm."

The ship lurched again.

"I am calculating for speed not smoothness," Kali said.

"I can do both," Kash countered.

The ship lurched two more times. The second one threw Lehana's hip sharply into the arm.

"Let him take it," she said. "Monitor closely and if he starts losing the line, take over."

The ship lurched again and then she saw Kash easily flow into handling the controls himself. His concentration was extraordinary as his hands moved smoothly across the flat starfield display on the desk in front of him. His fingers hovered above it tracing new pathways through the asteroid field. It was almost as if he was one with an unseen best line of navigation. The curves were smooth, yet the speed had not slowed. In fact it had increased.

A radiant smile took over his face. He looked as if he were basking in the most beautiful sunrise over a distant planet. Yet they were in the dismal darkness of deep space where the asteroids were closely clustered and the rocks were only a bit lighter than the void.

Lehana heard the ping of an active long-range scan. It didn't hit the ship. It hit an asteroid near them.

"Turn off running lights," Kash whispered. "It will make us a little harder to track if we aren't sending light into every dark space."

Lehana confirmed the command to Kali. Someone with this gift didn't need light. Whatever he was seeing was beyond her capacity to understand. Was it like this for him always? Like it was when they touched, seeing things no one else could; understanding and acting without conscious comprehension.

Kash remained in that state for the next eleven hours as they moved inexorably closer to the dead zone playing a game of hide and seek in the asteroid fields. They'd heard several pings along the way, but always a step or two behind their position. They were definitely being tracked. Was it Hellebor himself? Or someone else he sent?

When they came out of the asteroid field, they were in open space. No place to hide anymore.

Kash closed his eyes and slumped into his seat. "Returning the helm to Kali."

"You were accurate," Kali said. "And, as promised, more

smooth. I have recorded your trajectory choices for study so that I may do better in the future."

Lehana reached to touch him, then withdrew her hand. Right now, she could not take the chance of experiencing whatever it was they had together.

She checked her feelings for a moment. She didn't have the craving she had before. Was it because he was exhausted? Or was it just the passage of so much time? She shook her head again.

"Thanks, Kash," she said. "You have mad skills. Worth every DIC I pay you."

Kash nodded and slowly rose from the chair. "Sleep," he mumbled.

"Good idea. Get some shuteye while you can. There hasn't been another ping for at least three hours. I think we lost them."

"We didn't," he said. "I don't know how they are tracking us, but it's not with the pings. I could feel them slowing down when we slowed and speeding up when we did. They were not fooled by our game. But they aren't ready to show their hand yet."

Lehana wrinkled her brow and held her lips together. She wanted to deny that he could possibly know that. But given what she'd just witnessed she trusted it was true.

"Kali, scan the ship for trackers," she instructed. "Go on, Kash. We'll wake you if we need you."

He nodded and shuffled slowly off the bridge toward the hall leading to his quarters.

"There are no trackers attached anywhere to this ship. I have scanned thousands of times since we left Ydro-Down."

"Then where else might they be?"

"Unknown," Kali responded.

"Summon Adira," Lehana instructed. "If anyone knows of

tracking mechanisms she will. QueCorp is a master at tracking shipments…" The qubition! Was it possible they were being tracked with the qubition? But how?

She took off running toward the cargo hold. Push jockeys knew things, shared secrets within their clan. Even if it was a rumor, she wanted to hear it. "Erik, Kire," she yelled as she knocked on their doors. "I need your help."

They each peered at her through bleary eyes and barely opaque sleepwear.

"Are you aware of any way qubition is tracked after it's loaded?"

Kire rubbed at her eyes and yawned. "Some companies put a failsafe warning at the bottom of each crate. It only goes off if the load isn't delivered on the date agreed in the contract. When is your load due?"

"Months," Lehana said. "My contract with QueCorp gave me a quarter turn."

Kire and Aiden both stood straight and swallowed at the same time.

"Something wrong?" Lehana asked slowly. "You both look like you've seen a ghost."

"You did say QueCorp," Kire reiterated.

"Yes." Lehana drew out her answer. "I've delivered Q for them many times. I've always been on time. Always been paid. If there was a tracker I was not aware of it."

"You wouldn't be," Erik said. "Push Jockeys are sworn to secrecy when working on anything with QueCorp. I shouldn't even be telling you this now."

"And?"

"Stealing slaves means you are dead to QueCorp."

"And my contract is voided," Lehana finished the thought.

"Draaaaakh," she drew out the swear word. "So as long as I have the cargo, they can follow me."

"Exactly," the twins answered together.

"Is there anyway to remove this tracker?"

"Nope," they answered together again.

"It's embedded within the raw qubition itself," Erik said.

"And so small, it is as fine as a grain of refined qubition." Kire continued.

"The only way to find it is to dump out the qubition in space," Erik picked up. "And then, as it dissipates, scan for anything that is not qubition."

"Or just run from the location and ignore the dump," Kire suggested.

"Drakh! Drakh! Dakh!" Lehana stomped her foot with each utterance. "Do we know which part of the load has the tracker?" she asked. "I don't mind dumping the part where the tracker is and keeping the rest. But I'm not willing to dump the whole load. That's our money for laying low. It's our money for changing all of our identities so we can start again. I can't afford to dump everything."

"There is a tracker in every crate," Kire said. "With the amount of cargo you have that's thousands of trackers. You'd have to dump everything to be sure none were left."

"What the freeze?" Lehana swore again. "That freezing harami, DICs falling from vac of arse, piece of drakh!"

Erik coughed to end her swearing tirade.

"What?" she asked. "It's all true."

"And some would say the same of you," Kire said.

Lehana took a step back. "I'm not a harami," she said. "But the rest could be true."

"I assume you don't want to dump everything," Erik said.

"I wouldn't give that vac of…Ming…the pleasure." She paced

in silence for a minute then turned back to them. "We are going to deliver that load where it was contracted. That will get rid of the trackers and we will get the money."

"But hasn't the client already paid QueCorp?" Kire asked.

"Yes, but that won't stop them from paying again. They've been waiting for two years for someone to take this contract and I'm the only one who has ever agreed. They know that if they don't take what I have, it could be decades before there is any chance of finding a freighter big enough and a trafficker stupid enough to make the run."

She smiled broadly. "This is going to work out perfectly." Then turned on her heel and headed back to the bridge.

"Kali, look for a potential wormhole opening. We're going to Ignis."

"Ignis," Kali confirmed. "Calculating."

"Is anyone awake we need to remind to take the knockout pills?" Lehana asked.

"Adira is out with the drug in her quarters. Erik and Kire are taking theirs as we speak.."

"Stambuli?"

"Between sleeping and waking," Kali said.

"Inform her of our destination so she can make decisions about what to give the children and what to take herself."

"Awakened and informed," Kali announced seconds later.

Lehana took a deep breath and strapped into her chair. She scanned the bridge. Just as she liked it, alone. No one looking over her shoulder. No one second guessing her decisions. She felt a twinge of familiarity.

"Where's Kash?" she asked. The last thing she wanted was to do a wormhole jump with Kash onboard.

"Strapped in the med bay near his children."

"Awake?"

"He refused the knock out drug Stambuli offered," Kali stated.

Damn him. Though he wasn't anywhere near her, she didn't know if his presence on the ship would somehow reach out to her. But there wasn't a choice now. This was the best bet they had to get away safely and with a profit. He knew the rules. No touching. No distractions.

"Wormhole injection in one minute, twenty-two seconds," Kali announced and began her countdown.

Lehana gripped the arm rests of her seat, breathing with each second of the count down. *May it please the stars this goes smoothly.*

"No pissing in the vac," she said to Kali as a mantra against the storm of drakh that might meet them.

"Ten...nine...eight..."

Lehana counted in her head with Kali.

"Injection. Injection. Injection," Kali said as the wormhole opened and Lehana watched one load of qubition exit the ship and light up the cone-like passage in the wormhole. The ship went over the event horizon and spiraled down the hole.

Once again, she felt her body being stretched taut, her feet rushing toward the center of the hole. She gritted her teeth as the G force weighed her down. The ship counteracted that pull of gravity and she took a deep breath as the first flash etched the universe before this time in her mind.

She marveled at the Big Bang, the creation of stars and worlds, the colliding and exchange of materials, the violence of creation and its extension to today. Then things began to warp again as her body pulled in the opposite direction, the G force building while she prayed to the stars that ship would find its correction again soon. The other side of the hole appeared and expanded around her, swallowing her until she could see both the past and the present at the same time.

She quickly adapted to being being pushed outward as the future of the universe displayed with invitation. She gritted her teeth once more knowing the ship would compensate and soon they'd be pushed out the other end like a baby through the birth canal. It compensated, she took a deep breath, and screamed in fear.

Instead of spitting them out, the ship turned around again, pulling them back through the vortex. Back through history. Then it reversed once more. Three times. Four times. She didn't know how long Kali could keep up. How many times could she compensate for the gravity changes before they all died from the repeated crushing Gs?

Lehana's brain could no longer adjust. The pictures were spiraling out of control—future, past, future, past. There was no present. Her body no longer felt as if it existed. She could no longer feel or comprehend anything solid. She reached out to Kash with her mind but felt nothing. Noooooo, she screamed in her mind. I've killed him. I blocked him and now I've killed him.

This was the end.

The end of everyone's life on the ship. She felt a mistiness as if a veil was pulled over the universe, shutting her out from the stars; and her life's decisions were writ across the veil in judgment. Her pursuit of profit at all costs. Her pursuit of vengeance against Scraff. Her distrust of everyone and everything except herself.

She'd just killed everyone's second chance. She roared her distress. The children. She'd never have a chance to know what could have been. She'd killed their future. Her future.

She knew it as surely as she knew anything in this moment.

The mist turned to an ocean of tears. The stars were dripping light as they died out, one by one. She could no longer see the outlines of the ship. She was floating in nothingness, but without pain. She no longer felt the shifting Gs. Had she already died?

She gave into the end. No more caring if she was worthy of life. No more shouldering a burden she never wanted. She closed her eyes waiting for whatever final signal would transmit their death.

A human touch grasped her hand and squeezed. That one touch stayed the storm. The waves of tears, the circling in the wormhole, all movement coalesced into a single gentle wave led by a bright light; and the ship drifted on a smooth current out of the wormhole.

Ignis glared back at her through the view window, its fuming oranges and reds heating her immediately. She stripped down to a t-shirt and shorts, every part of her body begging for a return to the cool death of the wormhole as Ignis welcomed her back to hell.

CHAPTER 12

Kash's fingers still entwined hers. She didn't know if she leaned into him first or if he pulled her toward him. Maybe both. Her fingers traced the countour of his broad chest against the light shirt he wore. Needing to be skin to skin she raised the shirt above him until he removed it. She craved the coolness and rested her her head against his skin while resuming her exploration of him until she knew every ridge and valley.

His sudden intake of breath spurred her desire and her lips followed what her fingers had traced until his heavy breath enveloped her like a cool morning fog off a long forgotten lake. She wrapped her arms around his waist and buried her face and torso against his chest. She breathed in the welcome coolness, forgetting time and place as she naturally matched each rise and fall, breath for breath in her own thinly veiled breasts.

What she felt … what she wanted … was not the craving she'd feared before. Lehana was not compelled to be closer by some supernatural force. Yet she longed for more than breaths, more than heartbeats.

She wanted all of him—body and soul. Right here. Right now.

She turned her face upward, her lips parting in invitation. His blue eyes darkened further and she saw the depths of the Obsidian Rim reflected in them. Her breath suspended as the charged air pulsed between them, matching her heartbeat. He caressed her lips slowly with a finger, and then cupped her chin in one hand. Inclining his face toward hers, his lips lowered slowly until they barely touched leaving her lips singed with the heat of his breath.

Saturated with anticipation, her heart pounded in her ears and a feverish heat radiated from her head to her toes. She stretched up and grazed his lower lip with the edge of her teeth. Heat flared in his eyes and his rough hands cradled both sides of her face as he brought his mouth down on hers, hard massaging her lips with his and sucking the heat from her. His insistent mouth parted her shaking lips as his tongue darted in and out, sending wild electrical surges across her shoulders and down her arms leaving her limp.

He bent her head across his arm and lowered her to the floor behind her captains chair. He kissed her with such an intensity that she was forced to cling to him as sensations she had never known she was capable of feeling assaulted the world as she knew it. For the first time she wanted to trust, to commit, to have someone who would care for her like this always.

She wanted a good man. An honest man. A man that would suck the truth from her every day, challenging her view of herself and her worth. A man who could give her hope of recovering that feeling of the five year old child wrapped in unconditional love as she unraveled the tethers of her training with Hellebor.

As their lips sought more depth, they moved together in a rhythm of mutual understanding. Like falling into the worm-hole together, an abundance of knowledge and things worth learning about the human spirit opened before her eyes in the same way the universe had presented the past, present, and future in the transit to Ignis.

Ignis!

She clawed her way back to reality. They were on their way to Ignis. She had no time to wallow in lust or to explore the physical and spiritual pleasures Kash offered in abundance. She pushed her hand against his chest and reluctantly wrested her lips from his.

Kash hovered above her, one hand at the hem of her shirt. "Lehana?" His voice filled with a combination of dark passion and confusion.

She swallowed back the desire to finish what they started, to return to that feeling of total surrender; but the moment of absorption was gone. "Maybe we can get back to this after I deliver the Q, get the money, save us from Hellebor, and find a nice dark planetoid to spend a year or so on?"

He chuckled, lifted her shirt anyway and planted a languorus kiss between her breasts. "Are you sure?" he asked, his fingers tracing a slow circle around a nipple, followed by kisses doing the same thing before moving to the other breast.

She gulped as her hips raised to rub against him, pitting passion against reason. "I…uh…insist," she said on a moan, her body refusing to accede to her words. "Please, don't make this harder than it already is."

"Too late." With a moan, he levered himself up and stood, offering a hand to help her off the floor.

She refused his hand, knowing if he touched her once more her thread of control would dissolve in an instant and all logic would leave with the clothing they removed from each other. She adjusted her shirt to cover her once more and wiped her arm across her brow to push back the damp hair.

When Lehana felt she'd regained a modicum of control, she looked back at Kash. He was wrestling with getting his shirt back on. "You can leave it off...if you want," she said. She wouldn't mind him navigating the ship without it.

"I will if you remove yours," he said.

"Point taken." She licked her lips slowly. She wanted just one more taste of him.

"One minute, thirty seconds to Ignis station," Kali said.

"One minute?" Lehana's voice rose with consternation and she wrested her gaze back to her console. "Why didn't you let me know a lot earlier?"

"You left no instruction other than relay intention to dock at Ignis station and deliver cargo. That is complete. Do you wish me to wake the rest of the crew?"

"Yes," Lehana responded.

How long had she and Kash been awash in their own world after leaving the wormhole? It was all such a blur. Now, she couldn't even remember how it started. She'd have to be careful with wormhole transits in the future. Make sure nothing like this happened that wasn't planned well in advance. Planned so they had time left afterward to do...whatever needed to be done. To finish it.

No, she corrected herself. This is not a negotiation. Losing focus like that wasn't acceptable. Ever.

"Docking in ten...nine...eight...seven..."

Adira walked onto the bridge. "Did you fail to wake me for comms to Ignis?"

"I was a bit…uh…busy with other things after the wormhole transit," Lehana responded. "Kali handled it all anyway. Not as complex as Kollaiyar or other stations. It's only one small military base that is rarely visited."

"I'm going to check in with Stambuli." Kash strode to the door separating the bridge from the crew quarters. "Call me if you need anything."

"I will," Lehana said, not daring to look at him. She heard the door snick open and closed and the bridge felt suddenly too large and…lonely.

"Why are we here?" Adira asked.

"You know why, to drop Q, get paid, and get out of here to someplace where we can become unknown."

"I know that, but why the Ignis military? Why not some other place, a colony or something that can actually use the Q for ship propulsion or something useful."

"Because this is close to the dead zone and very few, including Hellebor, would dare to come here. Not to mention I can get the most in DIC payments here."

Adira paced near the comms station. "You do know the military here is literally dying for a chance to create more Q-bombs and get back their power. And you are giving them a chance at that."

"I'm not," Lehana insisted. "This isn't enough Q for them to make even one bomb. But it is enough for me to make five-hundred million DIC and save all of our asses from Hellebor if we can make it out alive and find a place to park out of sight for a while."

Adira turned her head away. "There will eventually be others like you," she said wistfully. "Others who will take QueCorp contracts and bring more qubition to Ignis."

"There has been no one for two years since the contract was

first let," Lehana countered. "Even if someone comes every two years, it could take a hundred turns before they have enough for even one Q-bomb."

"And that's why it doesn't bother you, because you figure in a hundred years you'll be gone. But what about everyone else?"

"The military interests have never made it into the Rim. It's a long way, and it may be a thousand years from now."

"Whether it is a decade, a hundred years, or a thousand, I care about the human race and don't want to see any of them subjected to any thing close to an Oblivion War again. If it reaches the Rim, where will we go? We don't even have maps of what's beyond. It's vast, deep empty space. Even wormholes won't help us if we don't know how to map a destination."

"Why does this bother you so much?" Lehana asked, surprised she hadn't noticed this idealism in Adira before. Had she not payed attention, not really wanted to know Adira more than as the savvy operator who could spew lies as easily as Lehana.

"Why doesn't it bother you!" Adira yelled. "Don't you care that you are giving poison to the biggest terrorists of five millennia? Maybe they won't develop more bombs in the next decade, but unless they all die they will find a way to do it. They're zealots. But people like you don't care. All you care about is how many DICs you can get."

Lehana bit back an immediate response. This wasn't the first time someone characterized her as a narcissist. It many ways, it was true. That was how she stayed alive, and it was valued by most of her trading partners. But was that enough for her? She'd vowed never to care about anyone or anything beside herself, and it had served her well. But now...now that she'd almost died in the wormhole. Now that she knew there could be something more with Kash...with...

She shook her head hard. No. She couldn't change now. She couldn't start questioning herself. The last thing she needed was to care about any one person. It was her responsibility to get this crew out alive and that took cold, heartless calculation.

"I apologize for yelling," Adira said. "You have been kind to me. You saved my life when you took me from Ydro-Down."

"I saved your life because you were useful helping me get the cat off planet," Lehana corrected her. "Not because I cared."

"Got it," Adira said. "I mean nothing to you except as a cat sitter and another crew member until you get tired of us all."

Lehana bristled. "That's right."

"Military greeting party at docking bay," Kali interrupted.

"Right," Lehana said. "Tell them it will be two hours before we are able to open the door. Give them an excuse, a repair that needs to be made, or whatever creative idea you can conjure. I need time to plan in case everything goes to hell all of a sudden."

"There are no repairs needed," Kali stated.

"I'll handle it," Adira said. "Are we still the *Mary Bowers*, or the *Phoenix*, or something else? The *Typhoid Mary*, perhaps?"

Lehana laughed and embraced the pointed name. "Sure. Why not be truthful about who I am for once?" She glowered at Adira waiting for an apology, or some look of regret, but it was not forthcoming.

"Only one problem, Ignis is expecting the *Phoenix*. It doesn't matter now that we know the Q is tagged with trackers," Lehana said. "Either Hellebor is already in the area or will be shortly. The good news is the Ignis military doesn't like him, so I doubt he'll be docking at the station and waiting for us."

Adira plugged into the public comms line. "This is the *Phoenix* informing you we will not be ready to open our docking doors for at least two hours. Our crew has contracted typhoid and it is not safe for anyone to leave the ship or for you to be exposed until our nanobots have completed expunging the virus from our systems and the ship."

Adira listened for a moment.

"Yes, our medic will provide proof that all crew are safe before anyone meets with a military officer," Adira responded. "Thank you for your understanding."

Lehana chuckled again, though not quite as confidently. "Sticking to a theme works," she said. "I might have said stomach flu or something not quite as virulent, but typhoid works."

Adira nodded but said nothing more.

Lehana watched Adira out of the corner of her eye, but there was no indication of what she was feeling. In the past she would have praised Adira for being strong, resilient, not letting anyone get to her. Now she wasn't so sure that was the best way to train crew.

The truth, as Kash would likely remind her, was that she did have some kind of feelings toward Adira. She was a likable person and had proven to be a great asset to the ship. As to compassion, Lehana wasn't sure if she could feel compassion. The moment of her decision to take Adira with her was about not wanting to kill the cat in transit. Adidra's story of slavery under Scraff did touch her in some way. But she couldn't honestly decide what part was related to compassion and what had more to do with justice for any woman who came within Scraff's grasp.

"Kali, call the crew to the bridge." It was time to make sure they had a backup plan if everything went tits up while she was negotiating the sale.

LEHANA AND KASH stood a foot apart with their backs straight, as if they were military officers themselves standing at attention. They both wore battle gear though their weapons were not obvious to someone looking at them. She expected a weapons scan and had planted a blaster for them to find. But her usual knife and tranquilizer dart were hidden buy a quantum camouflage vest. She hoped their scanner wasn't sophisticated enough to see through that camo. Word in the Rim was that the military was so focused on building up their qubition stores, that all money went to purchasing qubition, leaving nothing to other technology upgrades. She hoped the rumor was true.

"Sure you still want to do this?" she asked Kash.

"One hundred percent."

She hadn't really wanted him as her second, but no one else on the crew volunteered. Given the danger of just being on Ignis for even a short period of time, she wasn't going to force anyone to go with her. In fact, she was perfectly fine by herself.

"I won't blame you if you've changed your mind. I mean with your children and all, I'd understand. No judgment."

"I am thinking of them. I think of them all the time and every decision includes their welfare."

"Then—"

He interrupted her. "And your safety is critical to their welfare and to mine. Stop trying to push me away. It won't make you feel better and it won't make us any safer."

Lehana looked straight ahead. "Do you have the weapons we discussed?"

He nodded. "Easily found gilding gun, unloaded."

Air exited her nose in one huff. He had a personal problem with a gun that was normally loaded with chemicals that would painfully burn the skin off someone else, even an enemy.

Lehana didn't see it as a problem if it was used as a weapon of last resort. But she most wanted the negotiators to be scared, to know she had those kind of weapons and would use them if pushed. So, she relented to Kash's request to load it with a chemical that looked like gild but was in fact harmless, just in case the weapon was turned back on them.

"Zombie gun secreted," Kash continued. "Your sure the loss of memory isn't permanent?" he asked again.

"Positive. Stambuli says the dosage lasts about four hours. Plenty of time for us to be long gone if they get questioned under truth serum from someone working with Hellebor."

"Docking door opening," Kali announced.

"Eyes straight ahead," Lehana commanded. "Follow my lead." She slowed her breathing and put a half smile on her face.

The door opened to a contingent of six soldiers, two officers —a lieutenant and a commander—and four protection grunts. Lehana offered her hand to the commander. "Captain Lehana Saar," she said. "This is my navigator, Kash Trider."

"So, it's real names, is it?" the commander observed. "You do know you are a wanted woman, as is this man and his children. We could throw you in the brig right now and commandeer your cargo."

"You could try," she responded with an emphasis on the word try. "You'd have to get through our shields protecting the cargo, my crew of fifteen highly trained and well paid mercenaries who are completely loyal to me, and then stop my AI from blowing up the ship before you could take it."

She didn't dare look at Kash who she hoped wasn't grimacing at the raft of lies she just told.

Lehana gestured for the military personnel to come inside. "Be my guest if you don't value your life. Or your lovely planet.

I'm sure you know how unstable and delightfully boomy ignited Q can be."

The commander chuckled uneasily. "I doubt your mercenaries are loyal to you. Your reputation is that you are loyal to no one."

"That's true. But I pay for crew loyalty at a very high rate. Ask anyone in the galaxy. I get the best crew because I pay the best wages and percentages."

"And your slaves?" the commander asked.

"They are not slaves on my ship," she responded. "I pay them like other crew. You see, when you rescue a slave from a place like Ydro-Down they will do anything for you. Kill anyone. Even put their life on the line for me. That is the kind of loyalty I can't buy. But I don't have to in this case."

The commander narrowed his eyes, as if attempting to assess where the holes were in her story. Lehana kept her eyes straight at him, her chin up, and her stance confident.

After a few moments of silence she said, "Are you going to take me to someone who has the authority to negotiate for this Q or shall I leave and you can test your ability to take control of my ship?"

The commander touched a comms unit at his ear and relayed some type of coded message. Kali intercepted it and quickly translated it for Lehana and Kash. Scan for weapons and remove them. If successful escort both to my office.

Without being told to do so, Lehana put her arms out to each side and her feet wide apart. "Go ahead and scan. See if you can find what I stashed."

Kash copied her without saying anything.

Two of the protection grunts moved forward. One stood behind her while the other used the scanner. He pointed to the spot where Lehana had stashed the blaster and the person behind her retrieved it and held it up.

"Drakh," she said with emphasis. "I didn't think you had technology to spot that."

"We are more advanced than rumors say," the commander said with a slight sneer. Then gestured for them to continue the scan.

"Nothing else, sir."

The commander stood for a moment rubbing his chin. "Strip her to make sure."

"Make one move to try that and you'll find your entire contingent and yourself either dead or incapacitated and this load of Q that you've been waiting two years for will disappear," Lehana said with her jaw tightly locked as she and Kash simultaneously turned sideways in a battle stance.

"Commander?" the person behind her asked.

The man chuckled. "You've made your point," he said as if it didn't matter whether she was stripped or not. "I trust our instruments. And that the five of you will watch their every move throughout their stay here."

"Yes, sir!" they all echoed together.

He gestured at Kash. "Scan him."

"A gilder," the grunt now behind Kash said with awe. "I haven't seen one of these since my induction." He carefully handed it to the commander.

The commander slowly opened the chamber where the gel cap would be stored. "And loaded," he said. "Did you really think you would get away with this? What was your plan? To burn everyone at the negotiating table?"

"Only as a last resort," Kash said. "Only if you tried to cause us physical harm or refuse to let us leave."

"I could use this on you right now, then only have one of you to deal with," the commander said.

"It would be ineffective," Lehana stated. "We swallowed nanobots two hours before our arrival. Our skin sensors are deadened so we wouldn't feel the pain, and the nanobots would repair it before it took us down."

"There are no nanobots built to do that," the commander said. "We would know."

"Would you?" Lehana asked. "Who would tell you? You are hated throughout the Rim. You have no supporters with any power. Why do you think it's taken two years for someone to deliver this Q? Why do you think your recruitment levels are down? It's because everyone hates you at a gut level and would give up their lives to fight you."

"Everyone except you?" the commander stated.

"Oh, I hate you with every fiber of my being," she said, barring her teeth to add emphasis to the statement. "But, unlike Kash and most of my crew, I never let my emotions get in the way of profit. And the profit on this deal is temporarily buying my time to look the other way while we negotiate.

She stepped forward until she was within inches of the commander's face. "But be certain, if anything goes wrong and I or my crew feel threatened, my hate for you and all this planet stands for will override every regulator I have on my emotions. It will not be pretty. I was brought up by Hellebor and I know every possible way to kill people slowly and painfully."

She breathed through her nose as she looked straight at him and reveled in his slow swallow.

"No need to bring Hellebor into the discussion," he said his speech slow but still in control. "We know of your past relationship with him. We weren't sure you were still working together."

She threw her head back and laughed loudly, like she often did to show her wild abandon to frighten people. "We are closer than the best orgasm you've ever dreamed of having with a bevy of virgins tending to you. Once your with Hellebor you are his forever."

His eyes opened wide and he swallowed multiple times. The other soldiers coughed into their hands.

She pasted on the best wicked smile she had and looked him up and down. "I'd demonstrate but you aren't even a tenth of the man Hellebor is."

She stepped back noticed Kash in her peripheral vision. He stared straight ahead with his jaw locked tight.

"Are we done with the games now?" she asked, her tone serious once more. "Are we going to make a deal or shall I take my ship and leave?"

The commander once again spoke into his comms. She didn't need Kali's translation this time. It was obvious by the slump of his shoulders and him stepping a foot back that they were moving forward.

"I want two men in back," he said. "One at each side of them, and the Lieutenant and I will lead."

"Finally," Lehana said. "It seems that someone on this base actually wants the Q."

KASH LOOKED around the admiral's office while they awaited her arrival. He'd never been at a military installation. This room was even more stark than he'd imagined. No decoration to give rest from the straight lines of white and black like the bars of a prison. Even the stark white chairs were uncomfortable, as if there was never an intended invitation for anyone to sit.

When the generational ship he and his wife were on left Harmony Station two millennia ago, the Oblivion War was just starting to reach beyond the inner galaxy. Their entire ship's contingent were from the colonies that had protested the war and worked actively for peace. When they realized there was no hope, they all voted to go together for the chance to make a new life in the Rim. No one knew for sure they would survive, but it was better to die in the trying than to give up on the human race and stay knowing they would be dead soon.

He looked over at Lehana as she drummed her fingers on the desktop and bounced her crossed leg while looking at nothing. With all he had seen in the past few hours—the lies, the scheming, the acting—he was no longer certain of this woman he had started to care about. Was there any truth in her beyond the admiration for profit? How could anyone tell when she was lying and when she was telling the truth? Did she even know the difference between truth and fiction in her own life? What did it say about a person who could concoct a lie on the spot and make it so believable even Kash trusted it was true despite his own experience to the contrary.

He was no longer sure that the times she'd seemed to show compassion for him and his children were real, or if they were a way to manipulate him and his loyalty.

In the moment of their passion, after the wormhole navigation to Ignis, he thought he was experiencing her true self. She seemed to be without barriers and, for the first time, he was witnessing a truth she might not even know herself—that she longed for commitment. She wanted desperately to trust but had been brainwashed not to do so. He'd been sure he could see her heart in those moments. He was sure that with every deepening kiss he was touching her soul and, though deeply flawed with complications, it was beautiful and longed to be freed from the constraints of her upbringing with Hellebor.

He shook his head at his idealism. He hadn't yet considered where the relationship would lead, though he had harbored some hope it might lead to permanence for him and his children.

Now, instead of a memory of the taste of sweet honey, he had a bitterness in his mouth not knowing if anything he'd experienced was real. He wasn't sure he could live with himself if he'd made love to her and then learned it was all a game she'd contrived to manipulate him to do something for her in the future or, even worse, just because she needed to constantly prove she was the best game player in the galaxy.

CHAPTER 13

The admiral strode into the room. Her mottled brown and yellowish-orange skin was in bright contrast to the stark white, form fitting uniform she wore. The soldiers all straightened to attention and saluted. Lehana and Kash stood.

"At ease," the admiral said. Then she waved her hands at the four grunts against the wall. "You may leave."

"Are you sure?" the commander asked. "I would feel more comfortable having them here as protection."

She looked directly at Lehana. "You're not planning to kill me, are you?"

"No, Admiral. I'm here only to negotiate my delivery of Q to your base."

"See, no problem." The admiral waved her hand again at the grunts. "You are dismissed."

The commander bit his lip as the four men left the room. Lehana barely held back her chuckle at his obvious dismay.

The admiral sat across the table from her and Kash, with the lieutenant and commander flanking her on each side.

"Captain Saar," she started. "May I call you Lehana?"

"Certainly, and how shall I address you?" Lehana asked.

"Admiral Turgenov," the commander said loudly.

"I can speak for myself, Commander." Turgenov turned to look directly at Lehana. "As you are a civilian, you may address me as Admiral Turgenov or by my first name, Phillipa, as you have allowed me to do so with you."

"Thank you, Phillipa." Lehana smiled broadly, enjoying the discomfort of the commander. This was a good start, an offer of parity. Very few military men would even consider offering this concession. She pointed to Kash. "This is my excellent navigator, Kash Trider."

"And may I call you Kash?" Phillipa asked.

"Of course."

The commander wriggled slightly in his chair, his lips burst like he'd been forced to eat something very bitter.

"Let's skip the gamesmanship," Phillipa began. "We both know the truth here. I know you are wanted throughout the galaxy by Ming Waller for stealing his slaves." She stopped and scrolled through notes on her electronic device. "And a cat? That's interesting. And the reward for turning you in is a total of seventy million DICs. Care to comment?"

"I believe I'm worth a lot more than seventy million. As to the charges, on the surface they are true. However, I would characterize my actions as liberating the slaves rather than stealing."

"Noted," Phillipa said her lip quirking up slightly.

"And I know that your military is in desperate need of Q," Lehana said. "I was offered this contract two years ago and refused, as any sane person would do, and no one has agreed in the interim to deliver it. This means I am your only hope of getting Q for the foreseeable future."

Phillipa nodded with another slight smile. "And we both know that I've already paid QueCorp over a billion DICs for this load you are delivering and am not inclined to pay for it again."

"And we both know," Lehana took up the challenge, "that at the conclusion of our negotiations, you will claim that I never arrived and then demand a refund from QueCorp because they have failed to deliver the cargo. Furthermore, we both know that they will honor that refund minus the usual one-third carrying costs which will be borne by you."

"Point to you," Phillipa graciously offered. "I'm surprised you know about the refund policy as you've never purchased Q as a business."

"It is my business to know about the entire transaction at all times. QueCorp has been known to lie and cheat freighters in the past. As their primary trafficker I've had to know everything and make it explicit in the contracts."

Phillipa nodded in agreement. "You are as shrewd as rumored."

Lehana smiled, but said nothing.

"And what you told my officers about your relationship with Hellebor, is any of that true?"

"Yes," Lehana stated flatly. "I was indentured to him for fifty years. I learned my trade and his tricks during that time. He raised me from the age of six and was my mentor until the end of my indentureship. Our relationship was very close and he saved my life more times than I can count."

"And your relationship now?" Phillipa dared to ask.

The commander leaned forward for the answer.

"If you share the list of who you screw, I'll share mine," Lehana said.

Phillipa laughed. "Fair enough. No need to go into that level of detail in this negotiation."

"Exactly."

Phillipa turned to the two officers. "Leave us. I wish to continue this negotiation in private, without record."

"But…that's highly unusual," the commander said.

"Is it?" Phillipa asked. "Is it as unusual as you not recording how much you pay your pleasure boys and write it off as crew meals?"

The commander sputtered and turned red, but said nothing.

"Is it unusual," Phillipa continued, "that you always request to have a female stripped searched but never a male?

Lehana sent a long kick into the commander's shin and he yelped.

The lieutenant sat stone silent.

"Do I need to ask again?" Phillipa asked. "I said leave us."

The two officers scurried out of the room with the lieutenant keeping as much distance between himself and the commander as possible and mumbling, "I didn't know, Admiral. Honestly, I didn't know."

Once the room was secure again, Phillipa let out a long breath.

Lehana was impressed. This woman knew how to store information and use it whenever it served her. It probably is what kept her alive on Ignis. Zealots were an especially unstable group, and in the military those at the top were likely the most tied to the described ideals and sought the hardest to hang on to them.

But she wasn't letting on that Phillipa impressed her, just in case it was all for show. "Appears that you have a few problems in the ranks," Lehana said.

"Nothing I can't handle." Phillipa sat up straight and held

her p-tab in front of her. "Now, instead of each of us beginning at the top of the possible payment range and pretending we both care where we end up, can you tell me your bottomline offer?"

Lehana was liking this woman more and more. Did she always negotiate in such a straightforward manner or did she have a very well detailed dossier on Lehana that let her know all of Lehana's likely moves? She'd like to believe she could tell if someone was telling the truth by looking them in the eye, but Phillipa was as unreadable as anyone she ever knew—even Hellebor.

"As you seem willing to be truthful," Lehana said, "I will take you at your word. My bottomline is five hundred million DICs, not a single credit less. That is the best deal I can offer."

"We both know you have no one else who would be willing to deal with you when QueCorp will pay them more not to take a deal."

"They did that?" Lehana whistled in appreciation. "Ming really wants revenge."

"Do you blame him?" Phillipa asked. "Wouldn't you?"

Lehana tilted her head as she thought about that question. "I can be as vengeful as the next individual," she said. "But, in the end, I'm all about profit. Once I know I've lost, I can't see paying good money to stop a deal. When I want revenge, and throw away the lure of profit, it is for true harm. Killing someone I care about. Hurting me physically. Taking away the will to live from people who are barely making it. I don't see how missing out on a billion DICs in a corporation, where that is meaningless to their income, is worthy of throwing more money at it."

"What about justice?" Phillipa asked.

Lehana laughed so hard she could barely stay upright. When

she'd calmed she said, "Justice? QueCorp has no sense of justice. They mine qubition with people kidnapped from crashed ships or cast out by other colonies in exchange for discounts on Q deliveries. All of the miners are slaves with no pay and not even the bare necessities to remain healthy. QueCorp could well-afford to pay for employees or at least provide decent nutrition pills and medical care to keep them working. But Ming Waller chooses not to because he can.

"QueCorp cheats their customers at both the purchasing and delivery end, including the military. They bribe royalty to give them their poor for new slaves, and then pretend to cut the royals a deal when they are cheating them on the other end. Where is the justice for all those they harm?"

"Yet you do business with them," Phillipa stated.

"Did business. Past tense." Lehana held up her hand when Phillipa had something else to say. "I know. It wasn't exactly my choice to end my most lucrative contract. But I made choices knowing that is what would happen. Maybe I'm getting soft. Maybe I like to sabotage myself. Maybe I'm wormy from two many transits. Who knows? But what does all this have to do with our business here? Do you really care whether I'm a saint or QueCorp delivers synthesized milk to poor babies? I doubt it or we wouldn't be here talking."

"I like to know who I'm dealing with before I finalize a negotiation," Phillipa said.

"And?"

"And I've already deposited the five hundred million DICs into the Phoenix corporation."

"Of course you have," Lehana said with a note of disbelief. "And there is a hold on it until delivery. And within a nanosecond after you've secured delivery you will execute that hold and I'll be out my money and the Q."

"Check your accounts," Phillipa suggested. "No hold. Move it to a different account where I have no access."

Lehana quickly queried Kali. Indeed the five hundred million was there and Kali had already moved it to three different corporate accounts as was their usual practice on delivery of any cargo.

"I have one request," Phillipa said.

Lehana sighed. Now it was coming. There was always a catch.

"In order for us to believably tell QueCorp we never received the order, as you kindly suggested we might do, I need you to take the trackers and disperse them in the void when you leave."

"You hadn't thought of telling QueCorp you never received the delivery?" Lehana asked, truly surprised.

"I haven't had the years of devious thinking that you have. And my natural inclination is not to cheat anyone, unless they've cheated me. How much was QueCorp going to cheat on the delivery?"

"Just under three hundred million," Lehana answered honestly.

"Hmph. Then paying you five hundred million is a steal when everything is done."

"A fair deal for both of us."

"Will you take the trackers and disperse them?"

Lehana knew she could ask for more DICs to handle the trackers, but was it worth it? Though she couldn't conceive of a reason to ever return to Ignis or do business again, she could imagine a time when she'd run into Phillipa in the future and it might be worthwhile to have her owing something.

"How long will it take you to unload the Q and find all the trackers?" she asked.

"Less than an hour after you release the cargo to us. We will suck the Q through a sieve before dispersing it into our storage areas. It is fine enough to catch the smallest trackers."

"You've done this before?"

Phillipa nodded. "When we received our last delivery from QueCorp, eight years ago. Back then we were honest and had the trackers returned to them as contracted."

"Only an hour?" Lehana asked again.

Phillipa nodded. "Maybe less."

Lehana stood and extended her hand to shake and Phillipa accepted. "Agreed." Then she sent instructions to the twins regarding unlocking the cargo and helping to move it to wherever the military did this collection.

"One more thing," Phillipa said as Lehana and Kash had moved to leave.

Lehana turned back slowly. Please the stars there was not another catch. She was ready to be done and gone within the hour. Every minute on Ignis was likely a minute Hellebor was getting closer.

"It might be helpful to you to know who delivered that Q to us eight years ago."

Lehana's heart skipped a beat. Why didn't she think to ask that? She'd only been delivering Q for five turns. Who could it have been? Which trader was crazy enough to face the heat and dangers of a transit to Ignis? If there was another trader, they would have taken the contract when she didn't.

Her eyes widened as the only possibility revealed itself.

"Hellebor?" she asked, struggling to keep the squeak of her voice out of the question.

Phillipa nodded.

"Does he know I'm here?" Lehana asked slowly. "Is he waiting on station?"

"He knows you were headed here," Phillipa said. "He is not on station, but he is in orbit."

"And he plans to intercept us as we leave." Lehana knew it the minute the statement left her mouth. "That would be the easiest way for him to take us down, before we get up to speed." She looked at Phillipa trying to judge if there was some other game she wasn't seeing, some other request she was about to make. "Why are you telling me this?"

"Because you care about more than just profit. Because you survived Hellebor. Because I sense that this mission for him is as much about revenge as the contract he has with QueCorp."

"How could you know that?" Lehana dared to ask.

"Because I was indentured to him as well. When I was freed I wanted nothing to do with his businesses. I joined the military because the rules weren't that different from working for him. But I thought it was at least honorable work."

Lehana's mouth was open so wide in astonishment she had to concentrate to close it. This woman with Hellebor? She longed to learn more. She wanted to tell her the work here was not honorable at all, but she didn't have time for that. And Zealots rarely listened to reason.

"We'll have to leave the cargo section here. We can't afford the mass on the run."

"That is acceptable," Phillipa said.

She turned to Kash. "Can we open a wormhole before we are up to full speed?"

"Probably," he said carefully. "If we do it together."

Lehana took a deep breath. She still feared the connection with Kash, not the physical craving but the connection itself and what it revealed to him. She'd already come to terms with the craving of consummation. That could be dealt with. But the spiritual connection frightened her—the feeling that he saw through her games and her shields, that he knew more about her than she did herself.

She'd just have to be more careful. She'd focus on the physical this time and try harder not to dwell in that spiritual place. She shook off her fears. She would do anything to save her ship and her crew. "I will help," she said in a whisper.

"But we don't want to be too close to the station or the gravitational pull will suck Ignis in too," Kash added.

"How far away from the station do we have to be?"

"Too far for Hellebor not to catch up with you." Phillipa said.

Kash stood. "We have to go."

She looked from him to Phillipa and back again. "But…"

"We have to go now. We have to let the crew know what's going to happen."

"Hellebor might follow you in," Phillipa said. "If you open close to here and he is in pursuit, he could follow."

"Then we'll do a double jump," Kash said.

"Can you do that?" Lehana asked, still unable to fathom everything that was unfolding around her so quickly.

"In theory," Kash said.

"You've never done it before?" she asked.

"Never had the need," he said. "With your help, I'm fairly confident it will work."

"Give me percentages," she said, just like she always did with Kali. "I need eighty percent or better."

He smiled. "Eighty-two."

"You're lying."

"Am I?" He smiled and it reached clear to his eyes. Once again she saw them darken with passion and the Obsidian Rim reflected back.

"I believe you," she conceded.

Then, without thinking, she ran over and hugged Phillipa.

That hug had so much wrapped up in it. Respect for another woman who survived Hellebor. Thankfulness for her straightforward negotiation. Fear for what was going to happen to her once they opened that wormhole. Whatever Phillipa's strange ideology had dictated, It was clear she was willing to die for her cause.

Phillipa finally pushed her away. "May the stars guide your journey."

"Lehana. Now."

Lehana took one last look, then turned and ran at top speed. She wasn't sure if she was running away from something or toward something. All she knew is she had to run. She had to run hard so she no longer needed breath. She had to run hard enough to pound out the confusion in her brain, to pound out the fear of a double jump with Kash, to pound out the crazy idea that she may one day also find a reason to sacrifice herself for an ideal.

CHAPTER 14

The soldiers delivered the trackers just after the twins released the tethers. With the docking door secure, Lehana immediately dumped the trackers in the garbage hold. The minute they were within twenty-five thousand kilometers of the event horizon they would dump the garbage. That would destroy the trackers and, with any luck at all, Hellebor would get garbage plastered all over his ship if he was following them. That picture made her smile.

"All systems are go," Kali announced. "Leaving space dock."

Lehana slid into her chair next to Kash. He was already glued to a monitor looking for a tell-tale weakness in the quantum wave near Ignis. Because of Ignis' location, there were all kinds of malformations in the area. She held her breath as he searched for the right one. One that might actually have a little stability.

"Got it," he said and passed the coordinates to Kali. "Locking in first jump to the outer ring on the border between Unua and Dua. When we exit the first wormhole, we will create a second one immediately and jump to the inner ring of Unua at Cayo. Tell the crew to take those knockout pills, we are going in now."

Kali relayed the message.

"Cayo?" Lehana asked. "I've never been there. What is it like?"

"It had been selected for colonization by the ship I took out to the Rim," he said. "It was charted as a good candidate for agriculture. Deep green canyons, plentiful water, and an atmosphere that appeared to be safe for humans without environmental suits."

"Paradise doesn't exist," she said. "But if it's close, I'll take it as a place to stop for a year or two." She confirmed Cayo to the AI.

May the stars guide our journey, she said to herself.

"Ready to do this together?" Kash asked, turning to her.

She nodded and stepped toward him. He stripped out of his clothes and sat back into his chair.

"Wait. What *are* you doing?" Lehana asked, her eyes wide. "I agreed we would share your shell, even sit in your lap. But clothed, not naked."

"Naked provides better skin to skin contact."

"Nice try," she said.

"I'm not trying to seduce you."

"Yes, you are," she said. "Look, I know we've been dancing around the whole sex thing. Honestly, I'm amenable. But...this is *not* the time. You need to concentrate fully on the transit. Both jumps."

"I've never done a double-jump," he reminded her. "Have you?"

She shook her head, unable to take her eyes off his fully muscled body. She'd known he was a strong man just looking at him, and she'd confirmed that in their last jump, when she was plastered against his chest. Now, completely nude, it was clear that his arms, his shoulders, his thighs…his… She looked over his head. This was absolutely crazy!

"I'm not asking you to have sex," he said. "That would be too distracting, unless we both agreed it was more comfortable than not having sex."

"Too distracting," she echoed the first thought. Sex was never comfortable. Exciting maybe. With him, probably exhilirating, maybe even mind-blowing. "Definitely too distracting," she said again as if she had to convince herself.

"Right," he agreed. "I'm asking for us to have skin to skin contact. I want us to be as close as we can possibly be *without* intercourse. The more we can connect as many surfaces as possible, the more easily we will share the power of navigation as we glide through both wormholes."

She closed her eyes and massaged her forehead with both hands. Her brain was feeling like it would explode and she hadn't even touched him yet. "I…just…don't… think I can do it," she said, though her mind was screaming *Yes. You. Can.*

He stood. "Let me help you."

Standing made it even worse. She could now clearly see every single inch of him. She closed her eyes, and blew out a breath. "Who knew getting naked was so hard. Why is everything with you so damn hard?"

He obviously struggled to hold back a chuckle. "I understand," he said quietly.

"You can't possibly understand," she said. "Okay, I'll do it. But I…I can't look at you."

Her nostrils filled with his scent and she was transported back to those kisses. She turned and swayed toward him. He placed his hands on her shoulders.

She jumped at the connection as electrical current poured through her.

Kash wrapped her up in his arms. "Don't fight it."

The light flashed and she saw the universe pass by her as if she was watching a media event. Was this the way it was always going to be? Every time they touched? Fighting for control all the time it was draining her will to be in control.

"It will calm in a minute," he said. "Tell me when you've adapted to the hum."

She swallowed hard but felt steadier wrapped against his firm chest. Eventually, she did reach a kind of acceptable equilibrium. The low hum continued to vibrate along every nerve ending, but the initial disorientation had stopped.

One hand moved to the hem of her shirt. "I'm going to remove your t-shirt now. You have to help me. I want to keep a hand on you so you don't cycle between touch and no touch."

She felt a little breeze as he lifted the hem slowly. "Can you put your hands above your head?" he asked.

She did and she felt it quickly pass over her head and her arms were free. She opened her eyes.

He was staring at her as if mesmerized.

"This is some kind of stupid drakh!" she said, angry with herself for being so scared. "What's wrong with me?"

She tried to step away, but he pulled her back. "Don't break the connection," he reminded her. "Or you'll experience the shock again."

She unbuttoned her pants and wiggled out of them as he kept one hand on her back. Then she dropped her underwear and did the same. Stepping out of both, she kicked them aside.

"Satisfied?" she asked angrily.

He put both hands on her waist and held her at arms length, his eyes traveling over her body. "Very," he replied, a smile slowly moving from his lips to the dimple on the left side of his cheek, and then to his eyes.

"This damn well better not be some excuse just to see me butt naked."

"It's not an excuse," he said. "I'm telling you the truth that skin to skin contact will increase our ability to navigate. We need to flow together, not work against each other. That means breathing together, matching our heart rate. Giving in to the sway of the currents of time."

He paused for longer than a couple seconds.

"What?" she asked, uncomfortable.

"Truth?" he asked.

She nodded. "Truth."

"I still appreciate the view."

She kicked out a foot and connected with his shin. His oomph was muffled between gritted teeth.

"You really aren't good at taking compliments," he finally said.

"Let's get this over with," she said. "I don't want us to still be standing here naked when Kali announces we are going over the edge of the vent horizon."

"Agreed." Kash pulled her with him as he backed into his chair again. He sat and stretched his legs out between hers. "Your choice, back to me or facing me?"

"Both have their problems. How do I have to sit?"

"If you straddle my lap and fit close to my torso, that will be the best contact. With your back against me, I'll wrap my arms around your front. But there won't be much for you to hang on to, except my forearms. Though I'll navigate mostly with eye movements inside the egg, I may need manual access to the p-pad if things get too complex."

"So your really suggesting…"

"The closer position is for you to face me. Then you can your wrap you're your arms around my back and I do the same with you. Like we're dancing."

"Yeah, lap dancing," she said. "This *is* all a trick, isn't it? A smart one, but you can admit it now."

"No lap dancing required," he said. "Lehana, this is the best way. Now which will be more comfortable for you?"

"Neither." She looked down at his face. There was no sign of leering or other body language suggesting it was about the sex. All she saw was patience. Acceptance.

"Ah hell, I'll face you. You said that would be the most points of connection." She tapped his leg. "Give me a stable platform."

He kept his knees together and feet flat on the floor.

She stood to the side of his chair, leaned on one shoulder and then pushed off the floor as she threw her left leg over and plopped onto his lap.

"There. That wasn't so bad. Just had to put my mind to it."

She wriggled to get a more comfortable placement and he moaned.

"Sorry," she said, through gritted teeth, as she noted a hardening ridge beneath her. "I didn't mean…"

His hands on her back urged her forward, closer. "Mold yourself to my torso."

She wriggled again to inch forward and he hardened even more. "Damn. I'm sorry. Really. Just trying to get in position here."

"It's fine. I'll handle it. Just give me a couple minutes." He gently pushed her head into his chest. "Match my breathing." He took in a deep breath and let it out slowly.

She felt his heart beat in her ear and she pressed harder against his chest as if asking him to breathe for her.

"Slower," he said. "Match me again."

She took deeper breaths and tried to relax, but every movement of his chest, every whisper of breath along her shoulders sent feverish waves of need down to her center. How could she ever concentrate when they hit the wormhole?

"Securing egg shell," Kali announced.

The shell completely enclosed them making it nearly impossible to move at all. She'd never shared a shell with someone else. It was very close.

"Event horizon in twenty-five thousand kilometers," Kali announced. "Ejecting trash."

She breathed in his scent and the craving for him doubled. She dug her fingers into his shoulders, and her heart raced. Too close. They were too close. She was trapped with no escape, no control over her body over what she might do. Her breath accelerated along with her heart.

"I...can't...breathe." She struggled to pull herself from him. She wiggled back and forth, fighting his firm hold. "Let me out. I can't do this I can't."

"Lehana, look at me." He loosened his hands so she could push back from his chest.

"Out...I can't do this. I'm going to pass out. Let me out."

"It's too late to open the egg." He turned her face toward him. "Look at me. Look. At. Me."

She looked into his eyes, her entire body shaking with fear.

He took her hand, and placed it on his chest holding it firm. "Breathe with me, just like you did before. Take a breath in."

She felt his deep breath through her hand on his chest and struggled to do the same.

"Now let it out."

Her breath came out all at once. Her heart felt like it would burst from her chest and splatter all over him.

He continued to hold her hand firmly to his chest, his other hand against her back keeping her upright. "Breathe." He took a deep breath in, and then let it out slowly. "Breathe with me."

She tried again. It was easier this time.

"That's it. Now again, slower."

She tried again, it was easier. In and out. In and out.

"That's good. Let's do it again."

Finally her heart started slowing. The pressure of his hand on her back, gave her confidence as she inched toward him again. He moaned and stiffened.

"Again." He took in a deep breath. "No need to hurry. Breathe."

With each breath, she inched closer. Four, five more times they moved and breathed together. Finally, she molded herself to him once more.

"You're doing great," he whispered into her ear.

She doubted that was true, but smiled anyway. This wasn't so bad. At least the feverish desire had dissipated during her panic attack.

With each new breath they matched perfectly, until she felt he was breathing through her and their hearts were sharing one chamber.

"Event horizon in ten…nine…eight…"

Lehana dug her fingernails into his chest.

"Hang on," he said, his arms tight around her. "Whatever happens, just remember to breathe and ride the waves with me."

This time the distortion was not as pronounced as before. Hanging on to Kash she felt that he was consistently solid, no matter what her brain told her was happening. As he leaned to one side she leaned with him and they passed into the wormhole.

When the Gs built it wasn't just her lungs that were screaming. They shared the pressure together, as if they were one person but stronger. They protected each other from collapse until the ship compensated for the gravity change.

The flash of the universe showed the two of them superimposed over one another. She couldn't tell where one began and the other ended as the history of the universe surrounded them in a large oval. It was as if they were ghostly pieces of information within a two-dimensional plane held together by tethers from another plane above them.

Then the view turned inside out and the past was replaced by the future. The Gs weren't as bad this time. Kash leaned into the center of the vortex and she rode with him as they both were birthed out the other side into a new three-dimensional star field.

A feeling of complete calm surrounded Lehana. She wanted to remain here forever. Floating with Kash wrapped around her, never having to hide herself from him again.

Kali announced, "Wormhole opening for jump to Unua sector. Injecting qubition. Event horizon in thirty seconds."

As the *Phoenix* accelerated toward the event horizon, her heart danced in the victory of conquering her fear of giving up control to Kash. The fever of desire welled in her, twice as strong as in the first transit, and she embraced it fully. She rubbed against him, signaling her need, her willingness to touch even more deeply than before.

He moaned and hardened quickly. "If you truly want this, you will need to surrender all control," he panted. "It is all or nothing during the transit. Once we fall over the even horizon I won't let go of control until we exit."

Her mind heard the word *surrender,* and she rejoiced in it. She'd already surrendered when she'd stepped into the egg with him. She'd surrendered again when he took over their breathing and it filled her with freedom.

For once in her star-forsaken life, she didn't want control. She guided him inside her. "I surrender," she whispered.

He moved so slowly she thought she would die of anticipation. She tried to lift up to feel him moving inside her.

"Come back," he said, his voice raw with need. "Let me feel you completely."

She did as he asked.

"Now, don't move," he said. "Maintain the connection just like this."

Her inner chamber worked him even though she remained perfectly still; and he groaned again and pulled her head into his chest.

"Your controlling. You need to make the choice to accept whatever happens. You need to make the choice to let us flow together. There is no you. There is no me. There is only us. Surrender control to the flow of the universe around us. "

Though the need built until she thought she would scream for release, she forced herself not to move.

"Ten…nine…eight…" Kali counted again.

With each descending number she felt him growing inside her until she couldn't tell where he ended and she began.

"Now," Kash whispered as they fell into the well. "Move with the wave of the ship. Stay with me and we will ride the crests and valleys together."

She closed her eyes and surrendered all her senses to space-time, to the us, as they rode from one side of the wormhole to the other. Her body leaned with him as he chose the angles of their ascent and descent and she provided the counterbalanace to keep their journey smooth and steady. As he ascended she descended. As he pulled away she pushed down.

She barely felt the G force pressing on her lungs this time as all sensation filled every part of her. She moved up slowly as she absorbed the past and then pressed down equally slowly as they slid into the future. Wave after orgasmic wave assailed her, carrying her through multi-dimensional space with ease.

As the wormhole began to propel them out the other side, Kash accelerated and she matched him stroke for stroke. Kash grasped her by the shoulders and held her tight against him so deep she wanted it to never end. She felt every pulse as he screamed his release and the wormhole emptied with him into the peace of unrestricted liberation.

"Unua sector," Kali announced.

Completely spent, Lehana couldn't move. She wasn't sure if she would ever be able to move again.

"Confirm heading," Kash whispered.

"Inner spiral arm, planet Cayo. Time to orbit, seven hours, two minutes, seventeen seconds."

"Bed," Lehana managed to say.

"Open shell," Kash said.

It slid open and Kash slowly lifted Lehana off his lap, scooping an arm beneath her to support her legs. She curled back into his chest.

"Bed," she repeated.

"I'm trying my best." He stood slowly, cradling her body against him. "Mine or yours?"

"Mine." She softly kissed his chest. "Bigger."

He chuckled and carried her off the bridge and down the hall to the captain's quarters. He held her hand against the palm reader until the door opened.

"Wake us in five hours," Kash said to Kali.

"Five hours," Lehana echoed as he lowered her to the bed.

CHAPTER 15

Kash tossed and turned. Though he was exhausted he couldn't sleep. After they'd showered together and stretched out in her wide bed, she fell immediately to sleep. He wrapped an arm around her and tried to sleep, breathing with her once more. But his mind would not shut down.

She was the most frustrating and complex woman he'd ever known. Though she was terrified at touching him again, she'd agreed and in the most vulnerable of circumstances. When they'd entered the wormhole, she rode with him adding her strength to his navigation, and the second time he'd been surprised at her willingness to commit to the closest possible connection.

He stroked his hand against her head. He hoped she didn't regret that when she awoke. His doubts about her character were dashed with her final actions with Admiral Turgenov. She was soft on the inside. She had compassion and, though she would deny it publicly, she did care about others. It was her training and upbringing that stopped her from trusting.

During the second wormhole transit there was nowhere for her to hide in the coupling. He saw her soul printed in the universe past and future. It was good. Perhaps not pure, but its core was good.

He sighed and nuzzled her hair. What he would give to make love to her again right now, without the pull of the wormhole. He wanted to solidify for both of them that being together was the right choice. She could count on him. She could trust.

In her sleep she pushed her bottom against him and wriggled. He smiled and slowly moved against her, unwilling to stop his natural responses. Maybe…

"Captain to the bridge. Captain to the bridge. All hands on deck," Kali stated loudly followed by alarms. Then she repeated it again.

Lehana woke quickly.

"My clothes. Where are my clothes?"

Kash cleared his throat. "Uh. The bridge."

She jumped from the bed and pushed on a drawer. Drawing out her normal ship wear she stepped into it quickly, then looked at Kash.

"Run to get into something decent. I'll meet you on the bridge."

They both pressed through the door to her room at the same time. Lehana ran in one direction while Kash ran in the other.

The twins stopped in their tracks when they saw him, just before he hit the button to his quarters. "Forget something?" they said together.

"Not awake," he mumbled and slipped inside his quarters.

LEHANA STOOD in front of the viewscreen. Hellebor hailed the ship and requested imaging.

Freeze that. He would not see her until she was in full battle gear. She pushed another drawer on the bridge to bring up her spare suit and quickly put it on over her skin suit. Then she pulled two blasters, a large knife and a gilding gun, attaching them to her suit in full view.

When the others arrived she told them to armor up. When she sent their image, she wanted Hellebor to see a battle-ready contingent.

"Pinging again for imaging," Kali said.

Lehana looked around. The only person out of place was Kash. He had a gun but was obviously uncomfortable using it. She looked him straight in the eye. "It's time to fake it. You need to be the mercenary I hired. If Hellebor sees any hesitancy in you, he will take advantage. You will be targeted as his first kill."

"Don't worry about me," Kash said, straightening and widening his stance. "I'm protecting my children, this ship, and you. I'll play my part."

She nodded to Adira. "Patch him through."

Though Hellebor was seated and pretended nonchalance, his oversized image still startled her. He was at least two heads taller than Kash. His thick longer hair reached his massive shoulders. He sat with his oversized bare chest and a sleeveless vest draped open, barely covering his shoulders. His gun belt was obvious at his waist. She couldn't see what he was carrying, but she had a good idea. He'd have a lot more lethal weaponry than she carried, and he had no compunction for using the ones that caused the most pain.

"Zallili. It's good to see you again." Hellebor stood, revealing his entire body from head to toe and the heavy weaponry he carried.

"I'm no longer Zallili," Lehana said. "You know my name now. If you want to talk to me, you will address me in the proper manner."

"Do you prefer I call you Captain Saar, or Lehana?"

"I prefer you not call me at all. For now Captain Saar will serve. What do you want?"

"You, of course." He stepped closer to his screen so that his already oversized person filled the entire screen with no background.

Lehana held her ground. According to Kali he was within one hour of closing on their position. But a lot could happen in that hour.

"And my crew?" she said. "Do you expect me to turn them over to you as well?"

"I don't care about the slaves you carry aboard the *Phoenix*. I only care about you. You are the one of value."

"I paid my debt to you over fifty years. You released me when that debt was paid in full. I owe you nothing more."

"You owe me for my ship," he breathed the word ship through his nose and she could almost swear fire came with that breath. Did he have an enhancement to scare people even more? She new most of his tricks. Intimidation always came first in any negotiation with him.

"It was a small ship," she said. "What's the price? I'll send DICs to your account."

"No amount of credits can cover the price of treachery to your mentor. Your life is the only payment that is acceptable." He leaned forward and bared his teeth. His naked chest expanded as if he was going to pound his fists on it in some type of war cry. "No one steals from me and lives. No one! The debt is your life."

Lehana stared at him, unmoving. There was no getting out of this in any easy way, she realized. She knew he wouldn't kill her. That would be too quick. No, he'd want to make her pay day after day. Assigning her tasks he knew she dested. Tasks that went against what little morality she did possess.

"Is it your plan to kill me then, or are you turning me in to QueCorp for the bonus and have them do the dirty deed?"

"QueCorp can piss in the vac. I only took this contract to find you. You've been clever in stealing and trading and getting your own contracts. I admire your business acumen. If only you hadn't started your business on the back of treachery."

"That's rich," Lehana said. "Treachery is your stock and trade. It is exactly what you taught me. Treachery, stealing, killing. Trust no one. Love no one. Be ready to kill your enemies and your apparent friends. That was your mentoring and I learned it very well."

Hellebor stood and yelled, "I expected loyalty! For fifty years of mentoring I expected loyalty. I never let you down. Not once."

"Rule number four: No loyalty," she yelled back, matching his anger. "You pounded that into me day in and day out. If I dared to get close to anyone in the gang, you would make sure they did something to prove my loyalty was misplaced."

They stared at each other as if they were in the same room, though they were hundreds of thousands of kilometers apart. Lehana refused to flinch. Show no weakness was another thing she'd learned.

"What you call mentoring," Lehana continued, "I call slavery. After fifty years I am freed with only the clothes on my back and a meager amount of DICs in my account. Not enough to buy even the slowest interplanetary cruiser."

"Then steal a ship," he roared.

"I did," she roared back. "Yours! And it wasn't your freighter or your shuttle or even your ship with the QED drive. It was a stupid luxury cruiser. The one you should have missed the least. You should have been complimented I took your ship. Any other ship would have been too easy. But it was yours I chose to take because I knew you barely used it. What was it to you to lose that one ship in you fleet?"

"It. Was. Mine!" Hellebor ennunicated each word as if she was too dimwitted to understand her error.

"What are your terms?" she asked him, with a flick of her hand and a turn of her head, her voice now lowered as if it didn't matter what he said.

"You have two choices. The easiest is that you can dock your ship with mine. I'll take you aboard my ship and leave your crew alone. Given your lack of loyalty I doubt any one of them will come looking for you."

He waited a beat and scanned the others. No one moved and she silently applauded them for that.

"And the second choice?" she asked, pretty sure what it was.

"I'll blow you and your ship into tiny pieces."

That was what Lehana had expected him to say, and she knew he'd do it, too. There was never a half way with Hellebor. She might be able to buy a couple hours, but in the end she knew, even if they jumped twice again, he'd find them.

"Why am I not surprised at these terms?"

"Then why play this game?" He loosed the blaster from his waist and put it on the desk in front of him. "All you need to do is agree to docking with me and turning yourself over. You have my word that your crew can then go on their way, alive."

In spite of all his past cheating, stealing, and double-dealing, she did trust that he would let her crew go. Pirates—at least pirates that lived very long—did have a code of honor when it came to giving their word.

"May I have a few minutes?"

He laughed loudly."Don't bother planning another jump, let me save your crew some qubition in the eventuality you let them live. I can track you anywhere in the galaxy. That double jump you did had to be painful for everyone. I've not known another ship to survive that. I only had to wait until you were in a sector for longer than ten minutes to find you. The minute you were out of the second wormhole I knew your location."

She didn't doubt he'd managed to get some type of tracker aboard this ship. Whatever it was, it was a technology Kali couldn't scan. She needed to find where it was and disable it before they attempted any escape plan.

"If you jump without me, the next time I find you there will be no choice. I'll simply kill you all and you won't know the blast is coming until it's too late. I'll be there in thirty-eight minutes. This time you have the chance to make the right decision." Then he cut the comms feed from his end.

Lehana stood still for a few moments consciously breathing and slowing her heart rate. When she turned to face the crew, no one said a thing but it was clear they were all scared. Only Kash looked unchanged. His eyes were wide but his posture was stiff and his jaw held so tight that she wouldn't be surprised if he'd dislocated a couple of teeth.

"As long as he can track us, there is no choice here," she said. "No one could have followed us through a double jump without a tracker on the ship or with someone's belongings."

Lehana paused and looked at each member of the crew. She didn't want to believe that one of them would have agreed to carry a tracker. Certainly Kash and Adira would not. They were escaping slavery.

She stepped directly in front of Adian and Kire. "Did either of you accept something, anything for money before boarding my ship at Mùmín?"

The twins looked at each other with identical furrowed brows. "No," they said at the same time.

"You may not have known there was a tracker in something you bought, or perhaps someone slipped it into your case on station. Or perhaps something you agreed to carry that seemed trivial—a souvenir for someone else. I'm not accusing you, I just need to find it. Kali has scanned the ship and not found anything embedded in the ship with a signal."

"Nothing," Kire repeated. "We bought nothing, we carried on nothing but our own gear."

"Were your bags ever out of your sight?"

"No," Erik said. "We went directly from our rooms on the station to your ship. We didn't even stop for a piss."

"You are free to search our rooms, everything we brought aboard," Kire offered.

Lehana stood silent, debating a strip search of every room and every person.

"I…uh…may have the answer," Adira said. "I don't know why I didn't think of this before. Things have happened so quickly since we left Ydro-Down. It seems we have lurched from one crisis to the next."

"What answer? What do you think you know? No time for recriminations now."

"QueCorp puts trackers on all their possessions," Adira said.

"And that includes slaves?" Kash asked.

She nodded. "Especially slaves. I knew about mine because it was placed in me when I was forced aboard Scraff's ship. It took me a week to dig it out on my own and then another two weeks to recover from the infection."

"Where was it placed?" Lehana asked.

"In a place no one would think to look. Behind the navel, seated deep in the leftover umbilical."

"The median umbilical ligament," Stambuli said. "It's a miracle you didn't kill yourself digging it out alone. It's also connected to the liver and the bladder via ligaments and veins."

"Every one has this device inside them?" Kash asked again. "Including my children?"

"I don't know about the baby," Adira said. "But certainly your son."

"Knowing QueCorp it's your daughter as well," Lehana said. She turned to Stambuli. "Can you remove all of these safely?"

"Easily," Stambuli said. "I'll get started now. I'll start with the children as they will be quicker. Then I'll do you, Kash."

"You have less than thirty minutes," Lehana reminded her. "Can you get all three of them done before I have to leave the ship?"

"No," she said. "Not without another medic. Kash, I'll take you first. Yours will take the longest, but I believe I can do it in twenty minutes. If I don't put you under, I can stabilize you for the jump."

"I'll let Kali know she'll need to do the jump on her own." Lehana thumbed her comms unit and gave instructions.

"If we can dump the trackers, Hellebor won't be able to find us," Kash said. "This changes everything. There is no reason for you to go with him. We'll make the jump. Stambuli will remove the childrens' trackers and then we'll make the second jump before he finds us. We'll head to some planet deep in the Rim, regroup, get new IDs…"

"There isn't enough time," Lehana said. "We are now down

to twenty-three minutes. The timing is too dangerous. I'm not risking you, your children, the rest of the crew when he's so close. And there is no certainty that your trackers are the only ones. For all I know there's one in me too.

"Hellebor would blow this ship if he suspects anything. The only safe option is to turn myself over as I've agreed. I do believe that once he has me he will not pursue you—at least not immediately. Believing you all still have trackers, he'll try to use that knowledge to force my cooperation. He won't know you dumped them until it's far too late."

"No, I won't let you do this," Kash said.

"It's not your choice," she countered. "You don't control me. No one controls me."

"There's got to be another way," he insisted.

He took her hands firmly in his and she tried to pull away, but he wouldn't let her. She immediately felt the connection calling to her. Not the universe she saw and felt in the jumps, but him—the pure essence of Kash.

Lehana fought against it, but her fighting only pulled her further into the truth. She realized this was the last time she would see him. She would never know if she could really learn to love or trust. She would never know if she could be a mother to his children. She would never know, again, the joy of surrender—the joy of trusting enough to let someone else be in control.

She willingly moved into his arms. Without conscious thought, she matched him once more breath for breath, beat for beat, and she grieved that she'd been unable to let herself love him. He and his children deserved to have a free life. A life that wasn't living on the edge, filled with running, hiding, changing identities.

Stambuli placed a hand on each of their shoulders. "We need

to get Kash into surgery, or we won't get the tracker removed before the jump."

Lehana nodded, but held tight for one more moment. "I'll…be in…soon. I need to finalize some instructions with Kali."

Kash trailed his fingers down her arm and squeezed her hand once more. "Don't run. Fight!" he whispered and then let Stambuli lead him away.

CHAPTER 16

*L*ehana choked back the tears. It was as if she were five years old all over again. This was exactly why she'd sworn she'd never care deeply or anyone—she'd never love. Because the pain of losing it was unbearable.

She lifted her chin and looked at the three crew still on the bridge.

She looked at the twins. "Erik and Kire, prepare the shuttle. I'm *not* letting Hellebor board this ship. I'm going to meet him instead."

The twins nodded and ran off the bridge.

"Adira, would you like to go home?"

"I…uh…of course."

"I'm going to ask Kali to jump to Raeaa as soon as I'm half way to Hellebor's ship. I hope you will help Kash and the children settle there. From what you've described, I believe it is very close to the home he left."

Adira hugged Lehana. "Of course." Then she reached inside a pocket and pressed an ampule into Lehana's hand.

"What's this?" Lehana asked.

"My suicide dose," she said. "I always had it with me in case there came a time I could no longer take Scraff's punishment. I believe Hellebor will be worse."

Lehana held her apart and pressed the pill back into her hand. "Destroy this. Let it be released with the garbage of the past. You no longer need it."

"But you…"

"I *never* give up," Lehana said with confidence. "I survived fifty years with Hellebor. Don't count me out. I may suddenly show up on Raeaa in ten or twenty years and ask you to find me a home."

Adira's lip trembled. "You're the bravest person I know. Thank you for everything you've done for me. I'll never forget it."

Lehana straightened. "Yeah. Well, maybe you can name a cat after me or something." She pushed her toward the hall. "Now, go to the med bay. When Stambuli has removed the tracker in Kash, put it in the trash and it will be dumped in the wormhole when you jump to Raeaa."

Adira nodded, her bottom lip trembled and Lehana could see her eyes clouding with tears.

"Be happy, Adira. You're going home. You have your life back. Now go."

She waited until Adira left the bridge.

"Kali?"

"Listening."

Lehana's breath hitched and her vocal chords froze. She swallowed hard. "This…" She concentrated on steadying her voice. "This is the last set of commands you will receive from me."

"Shall I prepare a change of command ceremony?"

"I'm afraid you and I are at the end of our life as we know it," Lehana said. "I need a big simulated explosion. Something that would make it look like the *Phoenix* imploded. Can you do that?"

"Working on possible scenarios. When will this distraction be needed?"

Lehana checked the counter to Hellebor's arrival. "In about ten minutes."

"Compiling research and all possible scenarios," Kali stated.

"Here's the sequence of events that will occur. I'm going to take the shuttle out to meet Hellebor's ship. When I've cleared the *Phoenix*, I'll shift to top speed and aim it at him like a heat-sensing bomb. That should cause all kinds of alarms to go off in his ship, a good distraction. In the meantime you will be moving as fast as possible in the opposite direction. Create a wormhole as quickly as you can. Inject the Q, dump the trash with Kash's tracker, and then let loose the simulated explosion as you drop into the wormhole and get to Raeaa as fast as possible."

Lehana took a breath and looked at the timer again. She'd have to contact Hellebor soon or he'd be knocking at the door before her plan could execute.

"Once the crew is safely at Raeaa station, have Adira start parting out the ship to help support the crew living on Raeaa."

"The ship is to be dismantled," Kali confirmed. "Who will get me?"

"You choose. Put it in my final commands."

It took a good three seconds before Kali responded. "Thank you."

"Before you shut down," Lehana continued. "Make sure

everything relating to our specific journeys and transactions are destroyed. I want no one to know where we've been, any crew I've employed, or what I've done over the past twenty-something turns."

"I understand. I have a solution for the explosion," Kali stated.

"Good. What is it?"

"As the *Phoenix* approaches the event horizon I will use the gravity of the wormhole and the mixture of a second load of qubition with other present exotic elements in the hole to mold two disparate chemical attractions into a simulated q-bomb. With the pulsating pressure of the funnel, the simulated bomb will explode at the moment that the ship crosses the point of no return and the final release as the *Phoenix* is emptied into paradise."

Lehana tried to parse what Kali just described. The use of metaphorical language was not at all like her usual logic and clinical descriptions of process. In fact, it brought back memories she didn't want to have distracting her when she met Hellebor.

"That is…creative," Lehana said. "What data did you find to assure this will work without harming the ship?"

"The data was extrapolated from an observation of your interactions with navigator Kash Trider during the transit to Cayo. You provided an acceptable biological simulation of this process while traversing the information stream of spacetime. The combination of hormone release between two carbon-based beings under pressure provides a corollary to my proposed q-bomb simulation.

"The human simulation was explosive yet the two of you were not harmed in spite of increased levels of dopamine and norepinephrine in your brains.. The logical conclusion is that human experience is simply interpreted data in the human mind. That same data can be fed back to Hellebor and his crew by taking advantage of spacetime distortion when creating a convincing image of a q-bomb explosion."

Lehana consciously closed her open mouth. AIs were learning machines, but not sentient. Yet Kali appeared to grasp complex emotions, including hidden ones. She shook her head. No. She was reading too much into Kali's statements. It was all about chemicals and comparing thousands of pieces of data quickly.

"I suggest that if you witness this simulation in Hellebor's presence that you react appropriately to ensure the data is equally imprinted on his mind."

Lehana had to laugh. Whatever Kali had learned about human interaction was more than she'd imagined and now an AI was giving her advice.

She took a deep breath. She would miss speaking with Kali. In many ways, Kali was the only thing she'd trusted since leaving Hellebor's gang. Without emotion or guile, Kali followed her every command. Kali was the closest relationship she'd had since her parents' deaths...until Kash.

"Hellebor is demanding to speak to you," Kali said.

"I'll bet he is." Lehana faced the screen directly her shoulders back, stance wide, and her hands clasped tightly behind her. "While speaking with Hellebor, I'm going to give you a destruction command. You will confirm my command but not actually carry out the destruction."

"Understood," Kali responded. "Another simulation."

"Exactly. Open the channel."

"Four minutes," Hellebor said when his image was transmitted once more.

"Here are my new terms," Lehana said.

"The terms are already set. I am docking with the *Phoenix*."

"Kali, begin destruction sequence," Lehana said loudly. "Set to full detonation the moment Hellebor is within ten thousand kilometers of the *Phoenix*."

"Destruction sequence initiated," Kali said.

"Consider your choice, Hellebor. My terms or you get nothing and, if I'm lucky, your ship will be incapacitated by the blast. First, you will not dock with the *Phoenix*. I don't trust you not to steal something or do something to it once you are aboard."

"Go on." Hellebor waved his hand as if it didn't matter what her terms were.

"You will stay a minimum of ten thousand kilometers away from the *Phoenix* at all times during the exchange. I will take our shuttle across that expanse to dock with your ship. If you do anything to harm the *Phoenix* during my transit, I blow up the shuttle and me with it."

Hellebor roared with laughter. "Ah, Zallili. You have become a child, like the five-year-old I took with me. You actually care about these people. Or is it only one that one special person holds your attention? Which one is it, Scraff's concubine or the miner? As a child you had this disturbing tendency to fall the weakest of our gang."

Lehana said nothing. She didn't move at all.

"Which one? Man or woman?" he pressed.

"Hellebor is within ten thousand kilometers," Kali announced. "Destruction count down beginning. Ten... nine...eight..."

"Stop!" Hellebor yelled. "I accept your terms."

"Hellebor has backed off. Destruction sequence paused."

"Restart if he enters the zone again," Lehana said.

"You have three minutes to launch your shuttle," Hellebor said, his chest moving with big deep breaths. "Or you will know the pain of real destruction when I torpedo the *Phoenix*."

Lehana pressed the button to cut off the feed.

"Stambuli has messaged that Kash Trider is asking for you in the med bay," Kali said.

"No response. You have my instructions. Execute them exactly." Then she strode off the bridge toward the shuttle. No looking back. No what ifs. She was on the most important mission of her life and nothing would stop her.

ONCE THE SHUTTLE cleared the ship, Lehana looked back at the *Phoenix* one last time. It strengthened her commitment and she looked away. She stared into the deep dark of the Rim. She locked in the path to Hellebor's ship and hit the burners.

"I'm coming for you," she said aloud.

Three minutes and the shuttle would hit Hellebor's ship.

"Moving away," Kali announced.

Hellebor's ship pinged the shuttle. She accepted the audio, dropping Kali's feed into subaudible.

"What are you doing?" he demanded. "Slow down. You're moving too fast."

"Wormhole opening."

"You taught me that," she reminded him. "Just making sure you hold up your end of the bargain."

"If you ram the ship, I'll take out the *Phoenix*."

"Injecting qubition."

"You do and half your crew will be taken out by my collision. I've set the shuttle to explode upon impact."

"Event horizon in fifteen...fourteen...thirteen..."

"I'm backing off another ten thousand kilometers," Hellebor said. "I won't let you hit the ship. You know you can't slow down. What was your plan? Where were you going to find enough gravity to stop you for docking? Lehana, talk to me. You're no good to me dead."

"Second injection. Q-bomb simulation in five...four...three..."

A flash lit up all the space around her.

She screamed as if she was watching her parents being murdered again, then she cut the connection with Hellebor.

For a moment she stood numb, feeling nothing as her ship hurtled along its path with no destination. He was right. She hadn't considered how to stop the shuttle from hurtling through space. She'd planned to destroy his ship and her with it.

The crew was safe. They would be seeing Raeaa soon. Kash would make a new life there. His children would grow up knowing real love, knowing that their father sacrificed everything to save them...to free them.

Her chin trembled and she held tight to her control. She'd done everything right for once. She was a damn vaccing hero. No reason to lose it now.

She tried to take a deep breath as Kash had taught her. Instead, her throat tightened and her breath hitched. Tiny drops of water formed at the bottom of her helmet. She grasped the edge of the console, her fingers so tight she thought she could break them with the pressure.

I will not cry. I never cry. I chose this.

Gasping wails bounced back to her ears, amplifying the sound. Her knees grew weak and she slumped to the floor as her eyes bled tears of pain into her helmet. Her entire body shook with pulsing sobs pushing out what little air she had, suffocating out the life she'd seen with Kash with each breath she took.

She cried as her ship hurtled in space with nothing to stop it. She cried until the emptiness of the deep drowned in her own salty tears.

CHAPTER 17

$\mathcal{K}$ash watched Z-Huang as she ran after Eijaz, copying everything he did. Eijaz was surprisingly patient with her. They were playing hide and seek with the other children. When Eijaz found a place to hide, he held a finger to his lips and Z-Huang was perfectly quiet.

When they were found, she screamed and then laughed.

"Play again?" Eijaz asked her and she nodded.

Then another child started the count and the two of them ran to hide again. At nearly five years old, Eijaz wasn't very good at finding the best hiding places, but he was learning. He was healthy. He was free.

Stambuli said Z-Huang was doing well considering how long she'd been in cryo as an infant. Physically, she was doing all the things expected of an eighteen-month-old child and more. She could kick a ball, scribble with crayons, build small towers of rocks that seemed to defy gravity.

What concerned Kash was that Z-Huang had made no normal vocal sounds at all since they'd been on Raeaa. No cooing, gurgling, any of the initial speech formations expected of a baby. When most children were naming things and calling for ma-ma or da-da, she was silent.

Stambuli could find nothing physically wrong with her vocal chords. She told him not to worry. Maybe that was going to take longer.

But Kash did worry. He worried that being so long in cryosleep damaged her brain in some way, that she would never be able to speak or communicate her needs like other children.

When Eijaz had been this age, he would ask for things at least with a single word: drink, truck, more. And sometimes he would string several words together: mommy truck, me go.

Stambuli pointed out that Z-Huang was obviously learning and she wasn't mute. She showed emotion like laughter or tears. She screamed in surprise and in happiness. She stomped her feet or pounded her fists with the same type of temper tantrums of most toddlers. She just didn't use words to express herself.

Kash learned to play the naming game in reverse. Instead of expecting her to speak, he would say the name of something, like toes, and she would point to her own toes; or drink, and she would mime taking a drink from a cup.

Z-Huang waved at him. He waved back. A smile lit up her face and she toddled as fast as she could in his direction.

"Are you tired of playing?" Kash asked.

She shook her head and climbed into his lap. She curled into his chest and within a minute was sound asleep with one hand pressed over his heart. That one small action, which she did regularly, always hit Kash the hardest.

So much had happened for him to be here on Raeaa. So much pain and loss he still grieved. But he didn't want to pass any of that to his children. On the contrary, he wanted to protect them from pain. He wanted to protect her and Eijaz from a world where some individuals believed their desires were more important than the needs of any other human; where only a few individuals decided who was worthy to be free.

First his wife, and then Lehana had sacrificed their lives for a future they believed in but would never see. He would honor that sacrifice by using his substantial savings to free those he could from slavery.

Adira waved and walked to where Kash was sitting. "A message is waiting for you under your new name. It may be from the detective you hired to find Lehana."

Kash stood and offered Z-Huang to her. "Can you take her?"

Adira smiled and held out her arms for the transfer. "Of course."

"I'll let you know if I have any news." Then he walked swiftly in the direction of the community center.

Raeaa was a colony with little resources and they liked it that way. Without exploitable resources, no one wanted to steal from them, overpower them, or build large cities or factories. Though they had a space station and a small business welcoming vacationers into some of their homes, they were careful. Like his original home, Raeaa lived sustainably, advocated community, and did not tolerate violence.

The colonists also had a special skill with cats. They revered cats as equal beings to humans, and believed it was a sacred duty to provide them a home where the cats could evolve in their own way without hindrence or expectation. Every colonist had at least two cats living with them. Those with more acreage might provide care to a dozen or more. Colonists regularly reported that without a cat their human relationships, their very lives seemed to go astray. The presence of cats provided some type of special link for the colony that added another dimension of community no one could explain.

Kash loved living here. He loved raising his children here. Raeaa was more like the colony Kash had grown up with two millennia ago. He wanted Lehana to see it. He wanted her to know the life he'd lived now. How happy he was to see his children free. He wanted to give her the choice of choosing this life or another—no matter where their personal relationship ended up.

Adira and Stambuli told Kash to forget her. They said she was probably dead, that she would want him to be happy. But, if she wasn't dead, he had to be sure she was choosing whatever life she was living. He could not live with his conscience knowing she might be enslaved to Hellebor while he lived free because of her sacrifice.

When he reached the comms center, he tried to keep his hopes in check. The last time the detective had called, two months ago, they had a lead. But by the time Kash had followed up, she was gone.

It had been a year since the crew awakened to find Lehana had chosen to trade herself for their lives. They each had new names now. New identities and backgrounds had been created and perpetuated across all linked databases in the Rim. Thanks to the Phoenix Corp accounts, they all had sufficient monetary resources to live well. And Kash's own account was quite vast, thanks to compounding interest over two millennia.

"Hello, Kiran," the man at reception greeted him with his new name and pointed to the terminal behind him. "You may use that one. The message said he'd be available for twenty minutes for a return call."

"Thanks." Kash made himself comfortable at the terminal.

Within seconds the detective appeared on the screen. "I believe I've found her. But you won't like it."

Kash held his breath. Please don't tell him they found her dead. So many times over the past year, they'd had a lead that turned out to be false or Kash didn't arrive in time to locate her. Adira and Stambuli told him he should concentrate and raising his children; focus on the future not the past.

"Have you actually seen her?" Kash asked.

"Not in person. But my inside guy says it's her and that Hellebor and his gang are going to stay on Kollaiyar for at least a month of R&R. According to my source, she goes by a different name now, Tristan. And she looks different. But she has all the characteristics of the woman named Zallili who was with Hellebor for fifty years. Only this Tristan is even harder. Not a single soft edge to her. Her reputation is that she is as evil as Hellebor and enjoys every minute of it."

Kash expected she might have changed over the past year. She would have to in order to survive whatever Hellebor asked her to do. But he believed that deep down she would remember him. Deep down she would still be the good woman he'd known during their connection in the wormhole jumps. She would still be the woman longing for someone she could trust —someone who would always be there for her. He couldn't let her down just because it was hard to find her.

"Did your insider get DNA?" Kash asked.

The detective transferred a scan. "This is from a glass she drank from at a bar. You'll notice it's a one-hundred percent match."

"Send me the location," Kash said. This was the first truly positive proof she was alive and he wasn't going to miss his chance this time.

"Listen, I know you think you're in love with this woman, or whoever you think she is, but from what my guy tells me there is no way she'll fit into your life on Raeaa. I know the colonists of Raeaa can be idealists, but if you bring her back there, you and your kids will kicked off the planet faster than a shake. She's a thief, a con artist, and probably a whore for the right price. She fights to inflict the most pain possible on herself and whoever dares to take her on. She'll do anything for profit including killing if it fits her immediate needs."

"Give me the location" Kash repeated, his jaw locked. "I know what I'm doing."

"Okay. Sending it now. It's your funeral."

Kash transferred the information to his hand held. "Thanks for your help."

"If you do see Hellebor, don't mention me."

"I won't," Kash said. "As far as anyone is concerned, we don't know each other."

"Good. And…good luck." The man ended the signal.

Kash sat at the desk a few minutes longer. He waited for any second thoughts, but none came. He smiled and rose from the terminal. It was time to bring Lehana home.

"Good news, Kiran?" the man asked as he started toward the door.

"I think so," Kash said. "I hope so."

He returned to his children in a daze. Taking this chance would be as unforgiving as riding the wave through the wormhole. Only he had no gift for this journey. No practice, nothing to inform him how to prepare. He only wished he had Lehana's presence right now to keep him steady as he approached the event horizon.

KASH LOOKED to both sides as he walked down the alley. He stopped for a moment as he recognized the pleasure house he and Lehana had dragged the two men into. That had been the beginning of the end, when they found out Hellebor was tracking them.

Four more buildings and he turned the corner. He could tell by the constant churn of people in and out of the Hand and Snake Bar, that it fit the description of the place Tristan had been seen frequenting every night for the past week.

He swallowed the nanobot Stambuli had given him to counteract the effects of any alcohol he was served. He held his key to the door and it opened with a squeal as if the mechanics hadn't been maintain in decades. A wall of noise greeted him.

Lights flashed and individuals, in various states of undress, moved to music radiating from the center of the room. They rubbed against each other, gyrating and bumping, cloaked in a dirty cloud of smoke. Occasionally, wild laughter would erupt and overpower the pounding beat for a moment and then be reabsorbed back into the music.

The mixture of sickly sweet vapors, stale beer, and body odor made his stomach contract. He swallowed hard to keep anything from coming up. A woman glided between the dancers, offering a sharp-smelling drink. Each time someone held their credit key to pay, her floor-length semi-transparent dress moved like a shifting star field in a wormhole transit.

A carbon black bar curved into the barely lit room. Oddly shaped tables were placed randomly around the perimeter, each with a pedestal of either a hand or a snake. The bar itself had no stools, yet a variety of people lingered nearby, a few draped over it as if they couldn't manage to stand, let alone walk. A bouncer walked by the bar and pulled off two of the drapers and dragged them to a back door.

The starfield woman approached him. "Just arrived? What are you looking for?"

"What are you serving?" Kash asked, his voice hitching as he noticed a threesome in his peripheral vision publicly coupling. He couldn't help but stare as they switched positions without a care as to all those watching.

The woman looked in the same direction. "Does that interest you? I can make arrangements. Men? Women? Both? Public? Private? More than three?"

"No." He spit out the word between locked teeth. "Just a drink."

"Straight vac-alky or a special cocktail?"

"What kinds of cocktails do you have?"

"Whatever you desire. How do you want to feel? Sexy? Moody? Wild? Raring for a fight? The bartender has a steady hand with the right dosing."

"Straight vac-alky," Kash managed to get out, reminding himself that no one came here with anything wholesome in mind. Was this the kind of place Lehana called home?

"Key?" the woman said.

Kash held up his credit key and her dress twirled again. He felt like he might get sick.

The woman pointed to an empty table on the perimeter, one with a snake pedestal. "Have a seat there and your drink will be delivered. Peruse the menu. If you want company, complete the survey and you will be accommodated."

"There's only one person I want to see," Kash said roughly.

"Oooo. A repeat customer," the woman tittered. "Her name?"

"Lehana." He stopped, remembering that was no longer name. "Tristan. That's all I know. Tristan."

The woman's eyes widened. "Are you sure you have the name right? Tristan? The one who is with Hellebor?"

"Yes, that's the one. Is she here?"

"Not yet. She will be. She comes in every night with him. He owns her. He doesn't sell her to anyone. Are you sure that's the one?" she asked again.

"Yes. Just let me know when she arrives."

She laughed. "You'll know. Everyone knows when Hellebor and Tristan arrive."

Then she glided away.

His vac-alky arrived less than a minute later. He wrapped his hands around the vessel and took a sip. He grimaced at the bitter taste but forced himself to take another sip. He needed bitter right now to keep him alert.

By the end of his second order, his stomach was complaining and his head throbbed from the constant noise. He wondered if they would accept a large payment to stop the music for a while.

As if they read his mind, all the noise stopped at once.

A woman in hard black armor that fit her body like a skin suit appeared just inside the door. Her neck sported a thick, spiked collar. Her hair was shaved on one side of her head, while the other side had tightly braided strands of bright red and dark brown cascading down her back. In one hand she held a whip and in the other an obsidian baton.

She cracked the whip on the floor to get everyone's attention. "Where are the fighters? Let's get this party started." She walked around the floor with long, confident strides.

Everyone backed away.

"No takers?" She threw back her head and laughed like he'd seen Lahana do before.

"Hellebor," she shouted. "Pick one for me."

Kash held his breath as he heard the heavy footsteps from

across the room. Then the overpowering sweat of someone who hadn't bathed in a long time.

Hellebor hadn't changed one iota from the image he'd seen projected on the *Phoenix* more than a year ago. A large beast of a man, his mere presence sucked the air out of the room. He still wore the same open vest, his naked broad chest rippling with pure muscle and dirt, as if he'd walked through the dust of the desert to get here.

He joined Tristan in the center and held up his key. "I'll pay a million DICs to anyone who dares to take her on."

Whispers flew around the room, but again no one stepped forward.

"Five million," Hellebor said.

"I'll take her," Kash shouted.

He stepped forward and stood less than a meter from her.

Tristan didn't blink. She looked straight past him.

Hellebor squinted assessing him. "He looks strong enough, but I smell fear on him. What do you think, Tristan."

"No. He's too weak. Choose a strong man who can withstand my punishment."

She cracked the whip within inches of Kash's face, but he didn't flinch.

"You remember me, Lehana. I know you haven't forgotten."

"Forgotten what?" Hellebor demanded. "How do you know that name? Who are you?"

Kash stood tall. "I am slave 192 from Ydro-Down."

Hellebor pointed at Kash and roared with laughter. "So you live. The weakling had a trick after all." He grabbed Tristan's face roughly and turned it so she had to see Kash. "Look at him, Tristan. Your former lover is here. He wants you to come out and play."

"Scared. Weak." Tristan drove one end of the baton hard into his chest hard.

Kash stumbled back, but didn't fall.

"He'll die with the first real blow. What's the fun in that? Find me a real fighter."

"She doesn't want you. Go back to the cave you crawled out of."

"I'll pay for her," Kash said so all could hear.

Hellebor turned back. "Pay for what? To fight? Fine. It's your death."

"I'll buy her indentureship from you."

"She's not for sale."

"One. Hundred. Million DICs," Kash said with confidence.

The crowd gasped.

Hellebor walked a slow circle around the two of them. "One hundred million for one more fuck? Are you worth that, Tristan?"

She didn't flinch. She didn't speak.

"She's worth much more," Kash stated.

Hellebor laughed again. "Where does a slave get a hundred million?"

"I have resources."

"No matter. She's not for sale."

"Two hundred million," Kash said.

"No."

"Five. Hundred. Million."

The crowd gasped. Whispers spread around the room.

"I'd sell her for five hundred million," someone shouted from the back. "No woman is worth that."

Hellebor stood tall, each breath expelled loudly through his nose. The crowd quieted. He walked over to Kash, towering over him.

"One billion. Not a DIC less."

Kash stared up at him. Then he looked hard at Lehana. "Lehana?"

"I don't know you," she said without any inflection. "I am not the woman you seek. Don't waste your money."

"Seems she doesn't want you," Hellebor said. "Just because you buy her doesn't mean she'll fuck you."

"I'll pay your price," Kash said. "One billion credits."

Hellebor blinked two or three times. "Your lying. You don't have that kind of money."

Kash held up his key. "I'll transfer the money now."

Whispers went through the crowd again. "A billion. This is the best profit Hellebor's ever made."

Hellebor held up his p-pad. "Transfer it."

Kash tapped the screen and watched a billion credits transfer.

Hellebor looked. "Take her. You own her now. Do what you will with her."

Tristan screamed and ripped off the collar at her neck and threw it at him. He easily side stepped.

Then she tore off the layer of armor across her chest and threw it to the ground. She pounded on her chest."Is this what you want? Is this what is worth a billion DICs?"

Though her arms were well-muscled, the top of her body looked thin in comparison to the still armored lower half. A thin muddy-brown, sleeveles t-shirt was all she wore. Kash could see her arms were marked with bruises. Where the collar had covered her neck was a fire-red scar that was still healing.

"I don't care what you look like. What you've done. I know you've had to fight to live."

She continued to tear off more armor, throwing each piece

at him with more and more anger as she worked her way down each leg.

Kash planted himself, taking each blow without a sound.

When she got to the last one she threw it harder than any of the others and it hit him square in the chest. He grunted and rocked back for a moment; but then stood again. He'd had worse in the mines.

She now stood before him in only the t-shirt and a threadbare short. She held her hands out to the side. "This is what you paid a billion DICs for. Not the warrior. Not the strategist. Not the woman you saw in some idealistic dream. You spent a billion credits on nothing. Nothing real. Nothing substantial."

"I spent a billion dollars to free you from your indentureship."

"Free? Nothing is free in this universe. There's always payment."

Kash walked toward her and stopped within half a meter. "With me, you will be free to choose. I won't tell you what to do, who to be with, where to go. I only ask that you live free."

"Free to chose what I please?"

"Yes."

"I pleeeze," she drew the word out with sarcasm, "to remain with Hellebor. Am I free to choose that? Why would I want to go with a vac-for-brains farmer who would spend his entire life savings for a woman he can't fuck?"

Hellebor chuckled. "See what you bought. She's incorrigible. She'll make your life hell. But it will be your hell now, not mine. Tristan, you've put on a good show but it's not going to work. You're bought and paid for. A billion dollars. You've finally earned your keep."

"No. I refuse. Take me back. I'll pay you. I'll work harder. I'll work better."

Hellebor picked her up and threw her over his shoulder. He took four large steps to the door, then through her out on the street. "Take her and don't ever come back to Kollaiyar again or I'll kill you, no matter how many DICs you have."

Kash reached her quickly, he bent to help her up."

She rolled away from him with a groan. "Don't touch me!" She leveraged herself up and stood for a moment, testing whether her leg would support her.

"Let me help," Kash said. She was obviously hurt.

"You may own me but I won't let you touch me."

He backed away, his arms out to the side. "What do you want me to do, Lehana?"

"Tristan. Lehana is dead and buried. My name is Tristan."

Kash bit his bottom lip to stop himself from questioning her. Whatever had happened in the past year had made her Tristan. He had to accept that. "Tristan. I can do that. Now, please tell me how I can help you."

She stared at him, her jaw worked back and forth drawing tighter with each moment. "You don't get it, do you? I'm not something you can fix like a machine in the mines, or a child who falls down with a skinned knee. You can't fix what you've done. You've ruined everything."

"I don't understand."

"I never wanted you to find me. I never wanted you to put yourself at risk, your children at risk. Don't you understand? I gave it all up for *you*? I gave you a safe home for your kids. I arranged for Adira to take you to a planet you would love. I made sure you were safe."

"I do love Raeaa," he said taking another closer. "But how can I live in freedom when you live in slavery? How can I respect myself if I don't fight for your freedom too? How can I face Eijaz and Z-Huang every day knowing that someone I love is enslaved because of what she did for us? Now justice is served. The scales are balanced again. Now we are both free. Free to live. Free to love."

"The universe doesn't care," she shouted. "It doesn't have feelings. There is no database recording karmic points."

"I know that," he said, quieting his voice further.

"But you believe in balance. You believe in justice," she continued. "If that's true I can give you a list of all the places you can turn me in for a bonus. If you believe in karma then know this: I have only black marks on my record. Millions of negative karma points."

"That's not true, you gave up your life to save your crew. To save me. To save my children."

"One time!' she shouted again. "One damn time and you think that makes up for everything I've done. That is the one and only good thing I ever did. That's it. Nothing else. Ever! And now you've screwed that up by letting Hellebor know you're alive. He will come for me again. Maybe not this year or the next, but he will come. And when he does, he won't think twice about killing anyone in his way, including you and your children."

"And we will fight him again," Kash said. "We will fight him together."

"It's not just him," she said. "You don't know what I am. You don't know what I've done. Don't you see. It's not safe. You are not free when your running for your life."

"We'll find a way to make it safe. I saw your past and accepted it. I loved you as Lehana. I will love you as Tristan, if you'll only let me."

"You don't love me. Not the real me. You love the person I wanted to be, not the person I am. Whatever you think you saw in me, it wasn't real. It was a dream. A dream distorted in spacetime, in the heat of passion, that you fashioned into something more."

"I don't believe you," he said. "You're trying to keep me away, to protect me. But I don't need protecting."

"I can never love you," she said. "Can you live with that? Are you still willing to risk everything knowing that?"

He couldn't believe it. He knew her. She couldn't have changed that much. Not deep in her soul. He knew she had love to give. He knew she craved it. She just needed time to heal.

"It's true," she said quietly. "I'm giving you my truth."

"Prove it," he said. "Let me touch you. You know that when we touch I will know your truth and you will know mine."

"It's a dream," she repeated. "What we see when we touch is a dream. It's not real."

He stepped to within a few centimeters. "It can be real, if we will it to be so."

"Will is not enough. I willed myself to die and I didn't. I willed you to stay safe and you didn't."

Kash closed his eyes for a moment trying to understand what it must be like to put complete faith in the ability control everything, only to realize it was all an allusion. He'd learned as a child that the less he tried to control the world around him, the more freedom he experienced. He could never truly control another person. He could only work to control his reactions to their behavior. He could control the choice he made to live his life in peace and harmony with the universe no matter where he was, no matter what challenges faced him.

He opened his eyes and took in a cleansing breath, concentrating on the joy he felt in every transit in that moment when universe flashed that bright moment of clarity—when the past was let go and the present pushed him into the future.

"Tristan, I'm inviting you to be brave enough to try. No long term commitment. Simply try or the dream. Enter with me with no expectation of what will happen. No expectation of a dream or a reality. I invite you just to try."

"I don't know. It hurts too much to see what I can't have."

"Then let's just share in the dream for a while. Let's explore and learn. One day at a time. Each day you can choose if you want to believe, or just to dream."

"Each day?" she asked her voice only a whisper.

He nodded.

"I'll choose to dream today. Right now, this one minute in time. I can't promise anything beyond that."

He cupped her head carefully and lowered his lips, first feathering his kisses as the electrical current ran between them. The universe opened before him and he pushed it toward her as he deepened the kiss. With each plunge of his tongue the waves moved with him, forming a magnetic shield of protection around them as they pushed toward the event horizon.

Tristan replied in a dance of tongues, alternately exploring, sucking, seeking. Reveling in the dream.

When she pulled away, Kash lightened his own hold on her. His arms light around her but not clutching. His body sharing his warmth but not pushing desire. And he could feel her relaxing into lightness.

The universe widened, showing them their past, their present, and possible futures. The stars encircled them until they were once more traveling the waves together. Two separate stars in a sky of billions, but forever tied together by shared gravity.

For a few moments, they shone as the two brightest lights illuminating the path of all the planets circling the galaxy in the Rim. Then gravity pulled them closer and they chanced a delicate, temporary union. The explosion of energy illuminated their path through spacetime. The expenditure of energy inevitably tried to pull them apart once more. Hanging on to each other by the smallest gravitational thread, their individual lights were brighter than before as they traveled in parallel but separate journeys.

As their individual energy waned, gravity increased pulling them together once more. Circling ever faster, ever closer until the two appeared as one again, repeating the exchange of energy and explosions of light as they carved yet another path through the universe. Gravity pushing and pulling again and again as they orbited a sun only the two of them could see.

ACKNOWLEDGMENTS

As with every new series, there are so many people who are invaluable to the process. The Obsidian Rim series is unique in that it is a shared world and each author is creating books in that world. In 2019, that includes eight authors working together toward the best product that can imagine and write. Each of them has contributed to this world with ideas, research, questions, and spurred each other on. Thanks to Elsa Jade, Jane Killick, Shree Aier, Shona Husk, Sela Carson, Jody Wallace, and C. J. Cade for sharing this journey together.

Thanks for the passion you've shown for this genre, for the cooperative spirit in which you've entered and worked, and for the laughs when they were most needed. May all of you find the heroic energy to continue pursuing your dreams.

ABOUT THE AUTHOR

Maggie describes herself as an idealistic nerd with a romantic streak that surpasses any scientific explanation. Writing stories and making music has been a part of her DNA as long as she can remember. As a child she wanted to learn everything, and as fast as possible. She wanted to know how a car engine worked and what made people tick. She organized children to re-enact her favorite movies in the backyard and wrote stories and plays about worlds she'd never seen. She now writes in several genres but with a similar theme. She writes character-driven stories about *making heroic choices one messy moment at a time.*

Her love of life-long learning has garnered degrees in psychology, counseling, computer science, and culminated in an Ed.D. in Education. If she were independently wealthy she would probably add more education to include physics and cosmology and it's relationship to religion and faith. Maggie's past career pursuit included professorships and executive positions in academia as well as opportunities to consult in the U.S., Europe, Australia, and the Middle East.

Maggie and her husband have settled in the beautiful Pacific Northwest, in the United States, where she now writes full-time and invites her two cats to shepherd her throughout the universe.

facebook.com/maggiewrites

twitter.com/maggieauthor

instagram.com/mcvaylynch

bookbub.com/authors/maggie-lynch-875a4b99-667e-4237-bce1-25962e622286

pinterest.com/maggielynchauthor

ROCK RIFT: Edge of Sunrise
by Elsa Jade
Obsidian Rim Series Book 2

Chapter 1

When the call came down from the overseer's satellite, qubition miner Gavyn Grey's blood ran colder than the vacuum of space.

"Yes, sir. On my way, sir." He could've chewed through a mountain of slag with less effort than biting back the hatred in his voice as he toggled off the comm.

"They know," Arjay said tightly.

Not so long ago, it would've been dangerous to say even that much aloud. They'd had to play antiquated word games right under the guards' noses to disguise their coded conversations. But the clever engineer had been working surreptitiously to disable and redirect all the surveillance methods that QueCorp put in place to control their workers.

Gavyn had always known it was dangerous to rely on too many others, but he'd needed the engineer's expertise if they were going to survive. So far, his closest confidants had stayed true, although he'd never put all his Q in one ore cart.

But maybe the gig was finally up.

So close. So *freezing* close.

"I have to go or it stops here for sure," he said finally. "I'll take the chance."

Arjay drummed his fingers on the comm board. "It's always you takes the chances."

Gavyn nodded. "Since this is all my doing, it's only fair." When he pushed to his feet, the heat of the metal decking scorched through the worn soles of his boots. But even the planetoid's internal seething couldn't melt the stone-cold fury in his heart. "Besides, if they knew, they wouldn't bother contacting me. They'd nuke us all from orbit."

Arjay snorted out something that sounded suspiciously like a laugh. "And risk their precious qubition? Not likely."

"True." Q-bombs, powered by the wildly unstable element qubition, had been outlawed since the Oblivion Wars. Not like anyone on the Rim would waste that much power to kill someone anymore. A good old blaster plug between the eyes was just as effective, plus so much cheaper. And QueCorp was nothing if not cost-conscious.

Gavyn traveled through the older, shallower tunnels up to the surface base, nodding at the few miners he encountered along the way. With the whomper-dug shafts going ever farther and deeper into Ydro-Down's lethal mountain ranges, it could be days before he'd see some of his crew.

After the worst excavations, some were never seen again.

He clenched his jaw as he thought of his people lost in the darkness. But when he crossed to the space elevator cable that tethered the overseer satellite to the planetoid, he schooled his expression to blankness. While Arjay had circumvented the security measures underground, they'd decided to leave the surface systems intact lest their tampering be noticed. Management never went below.

In the small elevator car, despite his intention to remain aloof, Gavyn's skin prickled at the sight of the planetoid's stark, contaminated surface. If the company did know about the unrest, this would be their chance to eject him into the toxic atmosphere. Or wait just until he got above the light pull of gravity. They could pop the door remotely and vent him into space. He'd have fifteen seconds or so to curse them before he ran out of air and froze to death. Maybe he should've taken one of the old emergency e-suits from the surface base. But the bulky coveralls hadn't been serviced in many turns. Anyway, the real danger wasn't hazardous surface conditions or even the unsentimental void of space.

The real threat was other people. As always.

As the elevator zipped through the mesosphere, he had a brief glimpse of the transport docked alongside the satellite in orbit. The transport was an older model, not huge, but it had a quantum entanglement drive that could take it anywhere in the galaxy. Or what remained of the galaxy, anyway.

His people, who were responsible for finding and processing the dangerous ore that made that ship something more than a deadweight floating in space, made crossing the incomprehensible distances of the Salty Way possible. Ironically, most of them had never been off this rock.

Usually the transport carried away all the evidence of their hard work, leaving nothing behind but some nutrient deliveries and a soul-deep weariness. One way or another, that would change before the transport left orbit.

The elevator zipped into the satellite's receiving bay, cutting off his view of their one path to freedom. This time, for them, the ship represented a link not to the rest of the galaxy but to their future.

Stepping out of the cab, he took a short, sharp breath. The air was filtered, just like down on the planetoid. But somehow, it smelled different up here and it was always a shock. Not that he'd been here that often, not even a handful of times since he'd inherited the foreman position after the last explosion. He'd been so naïve, thinking that the flood of fresh blood might at least dilute the burdens on his people. But the overseer had brought him up only to show him how much time and material they'd lost in the explosion. And to explain, in exacting detail, what would happen if he let production falter.

"We trust you'll see how important it is to make right these losses." Overseer Harris Scraff had stared at him through slitted eyes. "We wouldn't want to have to enforce punitive measures for falling behind."

Gavyn had always known that their version of *right* and *trust* was far different from his own. The air in the mining tunnels might be sweltering, even toxic if the damps—the vapors of carbon monoxide, nitrogen, hydrogen sulfide, and others— weren't properly sequestered, but at least it didn't carry the antiseptic tang of profits drained out of someone else's sacrifice.

In the receiving bay, there was no one to greet him. There

never was. So he made his way along the corridor to operations. Since he was the only miner ever allowed on the station, he kept his eyes and ears open. Every time he went, he'd return to the surface to recall everything he could, sketching and notating, and Arjay was reasonably sure they could take control of the station along with everything else.

Arjay had no more confidence in the people then Gavyn did, but the engineer still believed in machines. To Gavyn's way of thinking, machines were made by people and so deserved the same level of trust.

Which was to say, none.

His heart beat faster. Just the lighter gravity, he told himself, and he hoped the specs for the transport were up on the board in the operations room. Knowing the schedule for its departure would be useful.

Not that his uprising aimed for the stars. He didn't aspire so far. He just wanted to let his people come up from the depths, breathe a little, share in the treasures they unearthed.

"Miner." The brusque announcement of his designation was part scorn, part command.

He understood well enough. He halted and turned slowly to face the other man. "Sir."

The guard sneered at him. "Overseer wants you in the ready room."

Gavyn hid his grimace of disappointment. Any little bit of detail he could pull from the command center would help when the time came. The ready room was nothing more than a place to meet with buyers for the ore. And sellers of the disposable hardware, software, and bioware that mined the ore.

He jerked his head in a nod and diverted to the ready room. The door was open, and through it was framed a view of the planetoid below. Since the satellite was locked in geostationary orbit to allow the elevator to move between the station and the surface, the view never changed, reminding anyone who looked down at the twisted, pitted hills just how rare and dangerous was their most valuable resource.

Although the elevator had been the likeliest place to murder him, Gavyn couldn't help the twinge at his nape as he stepped through the doorway, half expecting a drill screw to the tender part of his skull. Instead, he locked gazes with a woman, and the jolt that went through his nerves had nothing to do with rage or fear, although the sensation was equally primitive.

Ydro-Down had some women. Miners, support staff, other unlucky souls sucked into the outpost darkness. The monotony of peril and the toxic air corroded the shine off any potential desire. This one...

She didn't shine, not exactly, not in the matte black uniform of QueCorp admin personnel. But there was a subtle glow to her, like the strange luminescence of the rare, delicate coldfire crystals visible only in the terrifying moments when all the lights went out below ground. That was when a desperate miner, longing to see again, might stumble toward the light, knowing if he touched it, he'd extinguish it.

Beyond that first glance, she didn't move. Didn't smile, didn't even shift her weight in the way of most people first exposed to the sight and smell of a Q miner.

She didn't flinch in horror but neither did she reach for the pistol holstered at her thigh as most station personnel instinctively did. The weapon was company issue, meaning not a newer model, nor even one of the nicer ones when it *had* been new. But the way she stood with it comfortably at her side—not toying with it, not nervously avoiding it—made him wonder if she was an enforcer. Just what he didn't need on Ydro-Down: another spying eye.

She wasn't tall, maybe a meter and a half, which brought her barely up to his sternum, and she had the oddly slender but elongated bone growth of someone who had grown up in insufficient gravity with insufficient calories. The sleek cut of her chin-length black hair gleamed in the artificial lights like the fresh honed edge of a cutter blade. And the intensity of her amber eyes was even sharper in the instant that she met Gavyn's stare.

Then the overseer was talking and she half closed her eyes. The short black fans of her lashes felt like a signal to him, a warning. Of what, he didn't know.

Or actually, he *did* know, but if she or the overseer really had any inkling, his ill-advised revolt was doomed before it even started.

"Yumi Swinton," the overseer was saying. "This is Miner 488. He is the mine foreman and will be your primary contact as our new crew intercessor. 488's been foreman for the last two turns after an unfortunate accident. But he has worked here for"—Scraff tapped the info deck on his board—"ah yes, for his whole miserable life." The man smirked. "488, this is the new intercessor. All crew issues should go through her. But you know the drill." He sniggered.

Gavyn didn't laugh at the pun—it wasn't required. Management didn't need anything from miners except to dig. Their new intercessor stayed equally deadpan. Maybe she didn't think puns were funny. Or maybe it was the indentured servitude that didn't amuse her.

Sometimes the people who worked aboveground at a Q mining outpost were as desperate as the ones underneath. Though that didn't change the fact that she was the one with the weapon.

The new intercessor nodded at him. "Citizen. What is your

preferred title? Do you go by the numeric, your work title, or some other honorific?"

"Grey is fine," he started.

Scraff interrupted with a snap of his fingers. "488 doesn't need an honorific. He and the other miners are committed to Ming Waller's company until they work off their debt. It doesn't matter what you call them because most of them will dig until they die."

She turned that amber gaze to the overseer. "Except for the one who escaped recently with two children in cryo stasis," she noted. "He went somewhere, as fast as the Q could take him." When Scraff sputtered, she stood, still unmoving. "Citizen Waller hired me to improve production and reduce costs. To do that, I'll be working closely with Grey and the others."

"We don't work *together*," Scraff said with stiff reproof. "They do what we need, like any tool."

"I take good care of all of my tools because they keep me alive. Just as qubition keeps us spinning through the Rim."

Though a studiously blank expression had saved his life more than once facing the guards on Ydro-Down, Gavyn couldn't stop one eyebrow from popping up in disbelief. Her tone was as cool as his face usually was, but the words were as inflammatory as a pure oxygen mix.

And left him almost as heady.

He tamped down his response. Pique would only make Scraff more vengeful. Yumi Swinton looked old enough to have come from some other career, but she'd have to accept that she was obviously in a downward trajectory if she'd ended up running interference between Q miners and management. Under the best of circumstances, it had been a thankless position—caught between the excessive demands of the company and the realities of qubition mining. And for all that her serene stare left the overseer sputter-ing, her slender bones would crack under a single harsh blow, whether from an enforcer's staff or an unbalanced ore cart.

Not that Gavyn appreciated being compared to a tool. But he'd never deluded himself that the company thought any more highly of him than that—and actually, somewhat less. The brutal truth was, human life was one of the cheapest resources on the Rim.

The overseer's scowl was almost as bemused as Gavyn felt. "Talk to me in a turn about how well we should treat these tools." He flicked a contemptuous glance at Gavyn. "Slow, dull. A newly thawed cryoborn launched before the Oblivion War would be of more use."

The new intercessor inclined her head. "Until AI and robotics are capable of the instinct and delicacy needed to find and remove the ore, I suppose the company is stuck with mere people." For the first time, the corner of her mouth curved, not quite a smile. "And my contract says you pay me not per turn but quarterly."

Gavyn restrained a snort. She wasn't fazed by Scraff's blus-ter, and that impressed the freeze out of him.

Too bad she'd never collect that first paycheck.

When Scraff dismissed them with an angry wave, Gavyn stepped aside to let the intercessor pass through the doorway first, but she murmured, "After you," as she slung a standard-issue kit over her shoulder. The heavy weight didn't seem to unbalance her at all.

Fine. This wasn't a moment for some ancient concept of chivalry, dead even before Q-bombs hollowed out the galaxy from within. He didn't remember much from those old stories told in his childhood before he'd been traded into the servitude of QueCorp, and she had no reason to trust a virtual slave at her back.

Despite the thin soles of his boots, his steps rang with bottled rage on the deck plates as he left. Let her follow or not. Another set of company eyes on the surface—that hadn't been sabotaged by Arjay's clever engineering—was unfortunate but not an insurmountable problem. And she was bringing a weapon down to them, all unknowing. See, there could be a bright side to even a tidally locked dead moon.

She was so silent behind him that for a moment he thought maybe she *hadn't* followed him, and he glanced over his shoulder to confirm. Her gaze was parsing the close surroundings just as he did when he was here, but when he turned, her gaze flicked to his, the focus so intense he felt it like a finger tightening on a det cord trigger. Something inside him tensed, anticipating the inevitable boom.

But she only lifted one eyebrow in wordless question.

"The elevator is this way," he told her. "It's the only transportation to or from the surface. For us, anyway. There's also the EM catapult for heavy cargo, of course, and the ore transport ships, although those don't usually land." He launched a diffident probe of his own. "I assume you came in on that transport. It's not too late to jump it back through some wormhole to wherever you came from." He paused. "Although who knows how long it'll stay."

His unlikely hope that she would offer that information was dashed—as most of his hopes routinely were—when she gave her head a small shake that sent the sharp forward cant of her hair swinging past her wide cheekbone. "This is my mission now," she said softly. "I'm not going back."

He wondered at her word choice. Mission implied more than a job. But there was a faint lilt to her accent that suggested

Baseline wasn't her only language, maybe not even her first. Wasn't unusual for smaller, remoter worlds on the Rim to rely on their own patois.

He wanted to poke at that almost invisible crack she'd revealed in her self-possession. He was a rock-wrecker, after all; digging was what he did. But as quickly as the vulnerability had appeared, her expression blanked again, harder than a diamond bit. Harder than his own shields.

Walking into the tight confines of the elevator with her behind him made the length of his spine buzz. Which was ridiculous considering that most of his life had been a string of perils from cave-ins to starvation and worse. One small female at his back should barely register on his personal seismo warning system.

Yet once inside the cab, he pivoted to face her. For many people, a ride in a space elevator was an uncomfortable experience. Suspended in a coffin between earth and heaven with only a small encapsulation of breathable air was enough to make even hardened travelers queasy.

Yumi Swinton didn't blink, although as they descended, her attention shifted briefly to their view of the flat, excavated crater where most of the outpost's surface buildings were clustered. "So this is where it starts."

Was that a note of condemnation in her voice? As if maybe he should've swept up the ever-present dust before welcoming guests. "The most important part is out of sight, underneath." When her faint frown didn't change, he added helpfully, "The qubition. We might be small and spinning on the outer reaches of nowhere, but Ydro-Down has one of the highest Q-to-matrix concentrations of any qubition mine left in the galaxy."

"It looks like hell," she mused.

He wasn't sure if she meant to say that aloud. "Which one?"

He waited until her gaze angled toward him. "There are a lot of different hells. So I was just wondering which one you are thinking of."

"I suppose the one that resulted in the obliteration of most of the galaxy's citizens." She turned her back on the view.

The Oblivion Wars, she meant. "That was a long time ago. Ydro-Down was still an unmoored asteroid spinning aimlessly through space back then, before they hauled it into orbit here."

For the first time in their very brief acquaintance, her hand drifted down to the grip of her pistol. "Does hell stop existing just because we ignore it?"

That question was many designations above his paygrade. But then, his paygrade tended to run in the negative once QueCorp accounted for his cost of living—the cost of keeping him alive—on the planetoid's surface. Even though it essentially meant he'd never earn his way out of his clan's generational debt, he had to be impressed by the overseer's creative book-keeping. But since an indentured miner's life left him unable to match her philosophical ponderings, he kept his silence as they plummeted toward the outpost.

Or, as she apparently thought it, toward hell. But it was a hell he called home, and if everything went according to plan, damnation would come to those who'd enslaved his fellow hellions.

TRAITOR'S CODE: Freelancer #1
by Jane Killick
Obsidian Rim Series Book 3

Chapter 1

*B*rother Andre lied. His monk's robes were a sham, his documentation was forged and the reason he had hired me was because he was running from the Fertillan Guard. Blinded by the money, I took his payment, accepted him on board my spaceship and asked no questions. That one mistake changed my life forever and ended the lives of many innocent people.

Brother Andre was one of a handful of passengers I had agreed to take to Serilla. The passenger run was supposed to be an easy stopgap between more challenging freelance jobs and, apart from the need to be polite to everyone all the time, that's exactly what it appeared to be. The only novelty about the entire journey was the presence of a real, live chicken which a young couple had brought with them to present as a gift at a family wedding. The only gift the bird gave to me was the acrid smell of chicken poo which hung like damp in my cargo hold.

On arrival at Serilla, I held my breath as I walked through the hold to the controls that would allow the passengers to disembark. I thumped down on the panel and listened for the sweet groaning of metal as the mechanism began to move. Chinks of light from Serilla pierced through the cracks that formed between the doors and I stood in the breeze drifting in from the moon colony. It blew a wisp of my long dark hair from my face and I breathed deeply to take away the cloying clawing smell and reacquaint myself with the familiar tang of recycled air that had been re-breathed a thousand times by the overcrowded population.

Freddi, my one and only crew member, brought the passengers down to join me. He walked slowly, ambling with that lopsided walk he has, due to the accident which damaged his pelvis when he was an adolescent. It had stunted his growth a little, but it had not damaged his inner strength. What he had been through was enough for two lifetimes and the toll of his experience was etched into the lines of his face. Despite his suffering, he still had a full head of hair, even if more than half of its ginger strands had turned to grey.

He told the passengers to wait at a safe distance and I wrinkled my nose at him as he joined me at the controls.

"We're going to have to clean up in here when they're gone," I said to him quietly.

"By *we*, Cassy, do you mean *me*?" said Freddi. He frowned at me, but I saw he was smiling. Freddi and I had travelled in space together for a long time and he knew I did my fair share.

I glanced behind at the chicken which was staring out through the bars of a compact carrying case being held by the man from the wedding couple. Squatting down next to it, almost camouflaged against the dark in his black monk's robes, was Brother Andre. He seemed to be talking to the poor bird. Or maybe he was blessing it.

The doors fully opened to reveal the port of Serilla in all its ugly glory. Like most of the worlds in the Rim, the moon had no breathable atmosphere – in fact, it had no atmosphere at all – and so we had taxied the ship into a giant, enclosed, arrival hangar. Artificial lights blazed down onto the crowd of people milling about in front of us. There were crew attending to their vessels, officials in uniform checking documentation, traders and hustlers and probably pickpockets and criminals all jammed in together.

Through the centre of them all snaked a queue of arrivees waiting to pass through immigration. Freddi and I, being frequent travellers, paid a lot of money for a visa to bypass that indignity. Not the case for our hapless passengers.

With the ramp firmly extended, Freddi beckoned the passengers forward. Wide-eyed with anticipation, they filed out slowly. Only the chicken looked bewildered as it stared out from behind the door of its cage. A door which, I swear, looked as if it might be loose.

Brother Andre was the only one to stop and say goodbye. He clasped my hand between his palms and smiled. "It has been an honour, Captain Cassy," he said. "May blessings be upon you."

With that, he pulled up the hood of his robe and slipped discreetly into the crowd.

At that moment, a shriek rose from somewhere near the queue of new arrivals. Followed by a squawk and the sight of a very terrified chicken flapping its clipped wings as it made a doomed attempt to fly above the startled people below. It landed on the head of a woman who began screaming and waving her arms madly. The chicken was knocked off its impromptu perch and fell somewhere behind her. More or less everyone in the whole place was shouting and pointing and panicking. The crowd jostled, a handful of chicken feathers flew into the air and came back down on them like confetti, while officials in uniform waded into the whole mess barking orders about remaining calm which were totally ignored.

"How the vac did that happen?" said Freddi.

"I'm not entirely sure, but before he left, I thought I saw Brother Andre doing something near the chicken's cage," I said.

"The mild-mannered monk?"

I shrugged and continued to watch the chaos in front of us. Eventually, someone managed to grab hold of the bird and contain it. An official fired a blank warning shot into the air and the noise startled enough people to their senses to stop the panic.

"I better go out and track down some supplies," said Freddi. "We're getting low on... well, almost everything."

"See if you can get us another job while you're at it," I said. "Preferably one that doesn't involve chickens."

He laughed. "Aye aye to that."

I watched Freddi go and stepped back into the ship, only to realise I had left myself the unpleasant task of cleaning up the cargo hold. I sighed and tried to remember where I had put the cleaning materials.

But I never got to collect the cleaning materials.

The sound of boots marching onto my ship made me turn.

I was confronted by three men in the brown uniform of the Fertillan Guard. With the light of Serilla behind them, they formed three monolith silhouettes with the identical cut of their trousers, their jackets buttoned up to the neck and their peaked hats pulled down tight across their brows. The one in the middle stood a little in front of the other two and seemed to be in charge.

"Is this your vessel?" he demanded.

I felt the shiver of nerves go up my back. "It is."

"We have reason to believe you have been harbouring a fugitive."

"A fugitive? Don't be ridiculous!"

"We need to ask you some questions." He gestured to one of his subordinates who stepped forward to grab my arm.

"Hey!" I tugged my arm back, but it was held tightly in his grasp. "This is Serilla! You have no jurisdiction here."

But they didn't listen. I was dragged from the entrance and taken further inside.

I struggled and shouted and screamed at them, but my protestations were useless. There were three of them and only one of me: a hostage inside my own ship.

GRAVITY: CRYOBORN GIFTS
by Maggie Lynch

Help no one. Show no mercy. Stay alive.

Lehana Saar learned the smuggler's trade the hard way--as an indentured servant to the Rim's most notorious pirate. With the skills she acquired and now with her own ship, the star freighter *Phoenix*, Lehana is known throughout the Rim as a trafficker who will take any job, however dangerous, for the promise of a good profit. But when she's forced to crash land near a mining colony owned by the heinous, galactic cartel Que-Corps, she'll need all her cunning and experience just to survive. And maybe, with a little luck, she might even turn a profit by forging a deal with the mine's owners. That is if she can turn a blind eye to the dismal conditions and merciless exploitation of the thousands of Que-Corps' slave laborers.

Forty-five years ago Kash Trider and his wife crashed on Ydro-Down. Captured by Que-Corps, they were forced into the mines with no chance of release. Qubition ore killed Kash's wife and now only two things keep him going: his hatred of Que-Corps and the hope of freeing his two children from the same fate. When the *Phoenix* crashes near the mine, Kash risks everything to get his children on that ship. But will the hard-edged captain help him escape or will she turn him in for the five million DIC price on the head of a fugitive Que-Corps slave?

ROCK RIFT: EDGE OF SUNRISE
by Elsa Jade

With the accessible veins of qubition going too deep, the mining crew on Ydro-Down has two choices left: keep digging their own graves or revolt against their corporate overlord. Actually, both those choices will likely mean their end. But Gavyn Grey doesn't have anything left to lose, so he'll lead the desperate miners—reluctantly but relentlessly.

After an unexploded q-bomb left over from the Oblivion War wiped out her peaceful world when she was a child, Lumia d'Aspiring was taken in by the Order of the Last Candle, an anti-technology spiritual sect that trained her as an assassin, saboteur, and terrorist.

Infiltrating Ydro-Down to destroy the mining operations, she instead finds the wicked corporation trying to kill their miners —including the ruggedly intriguing but untouchable Gavyn

Grey. Should she help the miners end their tyranny? Or make sure nothing and no one survives the revolution?

After decades of desperation, Gavyn knows not to trust anyone. But the quick, quiet Lumia has skills his faltering revolution needs. Can he win her over—or force her to help? Will desperation make him lethal—or force him to trust?

Deadly battles and a possible traitor they can't track down are bad enough, but there's a strangeness at the heart of Ydro-Down they must unearth—and a danger in getting too close to anyone out on the Obsidian Rim.

A spaceship captain. A determined prince. A secret code.

Cassy travels the Obsidian Rim taking freelance jobs as captain of her own spaceship; but when one of her passengers dies from a knife in the back, she finds herself entrusted with a stolen code.

Containing secrets from the Fertillan royal household, it puts Cassy under suspicion of Prince Stephen, the attractive head of the Fertillan Guard. Battling pirates and evading arrest, Cassy unravels the truth hidden inside the code and realises its value to the whole of humanity.

As she gets closer to Prince Stephen, she faces a dilemma — can she trust him with information a man died to steal from his family, or must she turn her back on love to save the code for everyone living on the Obsidian Rim?

COEXISTANCE: PIPETTES AND PLOWS
by Shree C. Aier

After a disastrous laboratory accident, exobotanist Dr. Shay-laRam Gomez is desperate to redeem herself in the eyes of the scientific community, and more importantly, her beloved father. But now, with her carefully nurtured study of new black bean seeds in tatters, Shayla is banished to a dishonorable tour of the Obsidian Rim worlds with the man responsible for destroying her reputation – the brawny farmer from some backwater planetoid, Dr. Rahim Xie.

The people who freed Rahim from a lifetime of slavery are struggling under crushing debt to the Earth's Conservatory, and Rahim has vowed to save these destitute Prithvi and Rim farmers. He'll even steal classified research on sustainable crops from his irascible mentor Grumpy Gomez. When he discovers that meticulous Shayla has a hidden maverick streak, Rahim is tempted to enlist her aid. He needs more than her secrets; he needs her and her brilliant mind to help his cause. But how can he ask Shayla to join a revolution that will pit her against her own father – a man known for his political ruthlessness?

Forced together with their dogbot and humanoid companions, they'll travel to the edges of a decaying galaxy to fight the corporate greed that is slowly starving the worlds of the Rim. Are these scientists planting the seeds of their own destruction – or will their reluctant collaboration blossom into something beyond mere coexistence?

**Follow the Obsidian Rim series at
https://obsidianrim.com**